Id

Book I

This is a work of fiction. Similarities to real people, places, or events are entirely coincidental.

ID: BOOK I

First edition. April 11, 2023.

ISBN: 978-1734999013

Written by Michelle Marie.

For Sparky and Lulu

id

/id/

noun PSYCHOANALYSIS

the part of the mind in which innate instinctive impulses and primary process are manifest.

December

I will MURDER her...

Ha. How very Living Your Yoga of me...Seriously though bitch. Three days before you're supposed to be here?? Could this week get any better? I don't even know what bullshit excuse she gave me. I stopped listening. Whatever. I knew she was gonna flake. I knew it a month ago. I fucking knew it. I should have bought her ticket. It's my own fault. Now what? Now I guess I drive with that fucking dog alone. Not really an option...I have to go. And if I wanna see him first, I cannot put it off. Fuck. My. Life.

Oh well...at least the car is good. And for like 600 bucks?? Like I want to call it a gift, but there's a part of me that's like that mechanic knows he's never seeing me again...maybe he just pretended to fix the brakes. I'm gonna go with gratitude and it's a gift. Am I having a panic attack? I might be having a panic attack. Stop it. People do this all the time. Woulda been more fun with company but maybe it'll be empowering or some such. It's only four days. Weaker, dumber people than I do shit like this. Though they also cook meth...Frankly, it doesn't really matter how I feel about it. I've gotta do it, so let's stop this sniveling dragging of feet. Pack the car. Fetch the dog. Man up and fucking go.

On a side note...like he's ever really a side note...if Jacob Cutter pulls some kind of disappearing act, I will slit his fucking throat. He was so glib about the whole article thing...Let the lawyers sort it. Really? I mean it's just my name and my reputation. And on what planet am I gonna get a lawyer in the next 24 hours because some trust fund baby whose daddy bought him a job fucked up and pinned it on me? That's not really a legally actionable thing and even if it was, there's not really time for that is there...The sheer stupidity, dare I say arrogance of this cocksucker. The woman grants the interview on one condition and you cut the whole section? And then grab the laziest of headlines like a basic bitch...Fucking no-talent plagerist. Maybe stick to sports reporting. Whatever. He'll get what's coming to him. Just a matter of time. I just hope that I get to find out about it...Jake's tone though...pissed me off. I don't know why I expect him to get it. Or maybe he does and he's taking some perverse pleasure in it. Or he's a self-centered, immature man-child who was at the bar and doesn't give a shit...Am I a complete fucking idiot? Probably.

Alas, I love him. Really...Alas??? That's for real the word in my head. Like it's some Jane Austin novel. Whatever...it'll be what it's gonna be.

Is this fear? Am I afraid to do this drive? It feels like just regular old rage and annoyance...but realistically it's probably fear.

Big girl pants. I will be in his bed in 4 days. This is just a task.

~~~

Almost an entire day to get thru half of California? And not pretty California. Fucking brown and warehousey and gross. Of course it was the most perfect day today. Like that super green sunny perfect that annoys you because you took it for granted and never really noticed. The dog-sitter people were actually sad to see Diz go. Dude was like 'he was weird for two hours but then he was my constant buddy...' I should have left him. He could have had the lovely life. Seriously, could there have been a more idyllic morning? That shit was just taunting me...'Look how pretty I am. Why would you ever leave me for the east? You'll be sorry.' I never really thought I had it in me to be a Left Coast person, but now I'm not sure I will survive going back. Whatever. I made it to my hotel. I almost peed my pants when I saw the moose crossing signs. Moose? In goddamned Arizona??? Or elk...Who knew there were moose/elk in Arizona? Some big, not a deer animal. I had a full on 'it's dark' panic attack. The only thing that saved me from completely melting down was that the big ones don't dart like fucking deer. Oh, and it's freezing here too. I clearly don't have a handle on geography and weather. But now we're having drinks...me and Diz. I think a beer shouldn't kill him right? He seems fine. I'm getting the single-ish words, short answers from Jake. Never a good sign. Feels familiar in a way that I do not enjoy. Maybe I'm just on edge...but it's not like he's busy. Oh well...not a big deal. Two states to cover tomorrow to stay on schedule. Day One is a success.

Dude tho, fuck every stupid beige part of California.

Oh, and why—like actually why—is that Maroon Five pouring rain song on every station all day five times an hour...literally everywhere.

Whose dick did Adam Levine suck for that to be a thing??

~~~

Arizona and New Mexico are beautiful. Felt like I was driving thru a U2 video. Just me and the trucks. Weird, somewhat scary thing tho...Two independents—is that what they're called when there's no company name on their trucks?? I would swear they were stalking me. That's a lot of credit for how pretty my up at the ass crack of dawn self looked. But still...it felt like they were trying to box me in. I was a little freaked out, but there is some good that came from growing up with mountains...I knew I would lose them on the inclines...So I don't know if I was just being paranoid, but the fact that my cell also connected to some This is America network didn't help...Like AT&T just went away. It felt fake and creepy and Twilight Zoney. I've never been so glad that I have a big dog. And who knew this little bitch could break 100. Thanks Sweden.

Oh, and I know I shouldn't have, but we might have had a little sexy talk...Fucking boys...Think I'd learn by now. Panting in his ear is enough for him...Anyway, totally on schedule. I cannot wait to lay actual hands on him. If I was smart, I'd charge him for that...Alas...ha...Alas again. I really am anxious.

~~~~

That fucking cocksucker. Oh yes, he did sure as shit did call me in the middle of fucking Arkansas at 95 miles an hour to tell me he got the order to work this weekend. My ass. I don't even believe him. Like I mean, the military has been fucking up my life for so long, I shouldn't be surprised. I didn't take it well. I flipped my actual shit. Like screaming flipped my shit. Like beyond any normal human level of screaming. Like an insane person. Fucking Arkansas? I'm in fucking Arkansas—alone with my fucking dog, speeding like a maniac to get there without being trucker raped...I was insane. Like out of body. Screaming NO. NO. NO. You'll pardon me if I'm not in the mood to consider your feelings. That's too fucking bad. Tell them you can't. Do you know what I've had to do to make this happen? Tell them no (which is of course not a thing). I think I hung up on him. Or my phone switched carriers. I hate him so much right now. Though brightside: I made great time. Fury. I don't remember anything after that. I didn't even cry.

Til just now. When he went dark. And I can't drink because I have a finite amount of daylight drive time, and I sure as shit don't wanna make a home in this fuckhole. Hate. Everyone. So so so not yoga.

Ummm...also I'm not sure that I didn't actually call him a pussy...so that should work out well for me.

~~~

Fuck Texas. I was afraid to speed lest they think I was carrying drugs. That's a weird thing that white men probably never have to think about.

Or sane people. Also, why are there no hot truckers? What's the point of a truck stop?? If I was a truck stop hooker I would charge so much money...at least it hasn't snowed.

~~~~

Could Tennessee actually be trying to kill me? Is this the longest state in the world? I'm still not done with it. This day though??? I am absolutely done with it. I'm drinking. This trip is a cosmic joke. A big karmic fuck you.

Did your romantic ass think this was going to be fun, bitch? Nope...

Right about oh I dunno...Cocklick? Deersnot? Wherever the hell...I'm annoyed, but I'm not being cute (about the name), and I'm not that far off.

Rain. Pissing rain. Not at first. Not when my wipers were working just fine. Just a light mist then. But so dark. And then the passenger wiper blade broke loose...Like for real. Not just a little loose—fucking dragging across the windshield like a broken bone...and the only option to get off the highway was a service station across the road, or briar patch, or whatever they call it here...across the road from...wait for it...a fucking sex shop. On a dark hill. Two buildings. On a hill. In Tennessee. A gas station and a concrete block sex slavery prison. In the black rain.

Fucking horror show.

At least there was a lit pay at the pump option, so I didn't have to talk to a 'human.' And Diz must have sensed something because he started for real barking and snarling like an actual dog.

We're having thank god we didn't die beer...again...

And because why wouldn't the rest of it be enough—the check engine light came on just as I pulled into this delightful pet-friendly motor lodge.

I would cry if it wasn't so utterly ridiculous.

I might just drive over the next embankment I see.

And Cutter. Let's not forget him...is not speaking to me...so good on him for carrying on the whole gotta work thing, which is a lie but doesn't matter either way. I cant even muster the energy to give a shit.

Talked to the kids. They got a tree. God knows what that abortion looks like. But now, lucky bitch that I am, I'll be there in time to decorate it.

~~~

Check engine was only the gas cap. Radio silence from him.

~~~

Mommy made it. Yay Christmas.

~~~

So yeah, no Jacob's bed. And virtually no Jacob since. Christmas was successful for the children and kept surreal for me by 1) my period 2) Jon picking a fight about who the fuck knows what (probably my period) and leaving, and 3) a smidge of wine.

I hate it here already. The Land of Never Ending Townhomes. It's ok actually—the house. Not stunning, but ok in a contemporary paper timeshare sort of way. And it's like 30 seconds away from their school, so I should be feeling gratitude that Jon had a moment of sense and generosity. But I don't.

His house is like 35 minutes away. In truth it is closer to work, but also it will be super convenient for never being available in any real way in case of emergency.

In or out? That is the question. I will not be sidetracked by a fucking boy. He's gotten more than enough tears. That is all. Funny thing though...Maybe I don't love him. Want? Yes. Irrationally want. Appreciate, sure. Love though? Do I really want to continue to say I love someone who seemingly has so little regard for me? I'd rather not, but I don't know that you get to choose not to love someone...Never in my experience at least. He's a smart boy...if only he wasn't crazy smart and so pretty. But he's also insecure. And then there are the hang ups. Maybe not so much hang ups as he's not as open sexually as one might expect of a man who's slept with me for any amount of time. He obviously occupies too much space in my brain. Maybe if I stopped fucking documenting every second he enters it...

~~~

And he's back. I'm going on the seventh...He's watching his roommate's daughter for a month? I'm sure there's a story there that I don't really care about...So I guess we'll see.

~~~

I'm feeling much better. Survived Christmas.

I think I hate Christmas...When did that happen?

Oh well, now we move forward. Gotta send some email. Time to move.

January

God I want him...I stayed in bed an extra hour just to dream about touching him...super healthy.

I have to start looking for a job. Which is not a news flash. Not like I thought the money would last forever. Today, however I am obsessing over a table from Crate...

My fucking children are back. From school. Like an hour after they left. Apparently it's too cold for the busses?

The sun is shining.

Am I the bad parent in this situation?

Why would I ever think to check for a weather cancellation when the sun is out? I will now I guess. And why did it take an hour for them to get back? It's literally a half a block away...I guess we won't push jacking off til lunch anymore. That's a lesson. Two actually, if I count monitoring school cancellations when there is absolutely no readily apparent or valid reason to do so...Where have we moved?

I ordered the table. I'm obsessed. I have to go pick it up, which annoys me, but I'm not paying to ship a 5000 pound table because I don't want to learn a new road. And I have to put it together. It's only two pieces though. Surely I can manage that. And it fucking sold out in like ten seconds, so yay me not waiting with my thumb up my ass. Ugh. I hope I don't have to get on the beltway...

~~~

J-Day!!! Holy shit...I am freaking out...Jon is watching the kids, so I am mentally prepared for some sort of extortion. I've already been told that I need to be back by midnight...ummm. ok. You do remember how well I do with a curfew right motherfucker? And also...what're you gonna do if I'm not? Leave? I have to be somewhat nice though...at least until I find a real sitter.

It's a little over an hour. I'm going to watch him play hockey, like some fawning high school girl. Except I kinda am, which is sad. But whatever. This is a wasted exercise today because the only thing I can think about it what I'm going to wear. Is it too early to drink? I'm stupid nervous. And I'm not sure how this child will play into the evening...First things first, I have to get there...of course I have to take the beltway.

Can nothing just be easy with this one?

I'm wearing a hat...so cute.

~~~

I got lost on the fucking beltway on the way home. Driving in circles for like an hour. Not the highlight, but still annoying and of course I was late. I'm sure I'll be sucking a dick for that.

Anyway...it was awkward and kind of weird. Good call on the hat. I forgot that ice rinks are actually fucking cold. The kid was cute. Like 10 or 11 maybe...old enough to compliment me on my ensemble. At least someone in that house recognized...

It was strange. The sex was very sedate...almost proper. I think part of it was my not really being down to traumatize someone else's child. He was oddly detached from the whole night though. Like it was weird for sure, but he was like morning after sober stranger weird...Like I have no real choice in being here right now...I dunno...he did say that this isn't a great time of year for him, but blah blah blah...I was like puppy happy, so I made the appropriate concerned acknowledgment noises, but I didn't open up the full pity faucet. I'm never psyched to indulge the depressive, tortured genius thing when it gets in the way of what I want. And what I wanted was the beginning sex. Truthfully, we both kind of phoned it in. Stupid child. Who leaves their ten-year-old with a 29-year-old dude anyway? It's fucking weird. Not pedophile weird, just weird. Where's her mother? I feel like he may have said, but I wasn't listening...

I'm not sure that we're going to talk ever again. I feel like that was a goodbye. I felt it while it was happening...No sense dwelling. We'll see. If it was. And if I care. Today, I don't care that much.

And later he texted it was really good to see you.

Still flat. Still weird. Told the child I hadn't been feeling well. Note to self: vomiting and sex sound the same through a floor. Good to know. So we're still at we'll see.

And now that I've checked that box, it's time to find a job. I literally hate everything I see. Why am I even looking for editor jobs here? What would they even edit? HOA newsletters?

I'm in hell.

~~~

Overqualified for anything that interests me...I applied for one listed with an agency...They want me to come in and take a typing test... I'm sorry...The resume isn't enough? I'm not a fucking admin. Nope...Beyond annoying...but they're the gatekeepers and it's a super close editing job...so I guess we're going to get dressed and take a typing test.

He's been noticeably quiet...I've checked in a couple of times, and he responds...just nothing real...Do I care? A little. I have other things to do.

February

Ok...I may have just found my people. The work itself seems really boring, but I'm obsessed with the two chicks who interviewed me—Gwen and Melissa. Gwen seems to be the boss and Melissa (Mel) is the second in command. But when I said the only two things I hate are filing and breastfeeding they laughed. And not that polite, nervous shit. Like we're going to be friends laughed. It's not a real editing job. It's some kind of bank/money laundering watchdog thing, which sounds boring but the people seem oddly cool. Of course they are contractually obligated to pay me nothing for 90 days or some shit...Fucking agencies...But I love them. And I'm ahead of my financial schedule, so I'm going to do it.

~~~

Jon is going to come over to put the table together...and I don't have to get on the beltway!! And the pizza place Jackie has been screaming about since I got here is like next door...so yay for me winning again. Oh, and I went to their house last week-Jackie and Jim's...No, I am not joking. It's all very civilized and normal. She's become very civilized and normal. And I...am very glad I didn't listen to her and move there. Cute town, but it's like old, boring white people suburbia land. Nothing to do unless you want to get frozen custard every fucking day. OMG, and she's pregnant too, so...I'm not saying she's off the list, but what practical good are you to me pregnant? Husband is lovely though. We'll see how long she can pull that off. We certainly didn't tell any of the old stories...Which I guess is just how it is now. Probably best to just let those days stay buried. I'm not judging...I'm not sure that I'd want to subject my respectable new husband to them either. I wonder if she lied about her number...ha. Of course she did. Even if she was honest about the number, I'm sure she left out the combinations of a lot of those encounters. Not gonna lie, it does make me a little sad watching a whore go straight.

I have to drive up to some retirement thing for the old man. It seems kinda silly...He's never really going to retire. But it's at The Lakes, which is an odd choice, and they're never letting my non-white vagina in that club for any other thing...so while politically I am appalled, I am 100% fucking going. I hope it doesn't snow.

We've gone back to phone sex. He has zero interest in seeing me in real life. Apparently I haven't learned that lesson yet either. There's always some reason to cancel. Who's more fucked up in this equation? My vote is him obviously because at least I'm aware of how pathetic I'm being. And perhaps more to the point, no matter what foolishness I display, I'm always on my side...It'll do for now. Until I grow bored.

I do kind of hate that it does it for me.

Oh ha—they put me in an office with two actual male children, so I have something to play with.

And guess who just resurfaced? From Japan...That ought to be interesting. Testing the waters...I get it. It was intense. And I was insane. But he was the first after that void of a marriage, so of course I was insane.

Was. Ha. Like the past tense is applicable even a little.

~~~

Why oh why...do we pay taxes? Nope. I am about to watch some AbFab though. But why did I stop picking up waiters? Sure, marriage is a reason. But when I say holy shit...I mean 'holy shit, when did 24 year olds learn how to fuck?' That is a gift. So ridiculous...I can't quite get past it...If I had been an ounce more sober I might have Miseryed him, thrown him in my car and locked him in my closet forever...The hips...I'm not sure I've ever even noticed hips, but these hips were from some demon place. God bless youth. No real downtime to speak of...unless I had a little nap, which is entirely possible.

Oh, and this grown ass woman straight lied to her daddy. All-night bowling...Really? Not sure which is crazier—that I had the nerve to utter it or that he just readily accepted it. Something about being home that cues up high school I guess.

Well that, and I'm not sure we're cool enough for me to be like 'so dad, you know that cute waiter from your very public and well-attended retirement soiree? Yeah, he's going to come out with us in this very small town where I stick out like a sparkly thumb and then I'm gonna go to his house and fuck him until the sun comes up. Which is actually a really good thing if you consider it, because I'm not quite sure where his house is or how to get home from it.' Probably not in this lifetime.

Second-best lover ever. Objectively. Shocking. And polite. And considerate.

What in the ever living fuck just happened? Did I just have my world rocked by a kid? Am I about to be a psychotic stalker?

Speaking of...I don't care a lot today but just for continuity of documenting the crazy, I made it five days without checking up on Cutter. Straight logged in to Match. Funny. Happy hunting, darlin. Let's see if you can break the habit. Though once he fucks someone new, I'll be erased...If we're as alike as I think we are. New dick takes away the sting. Maybe he's looking for a new dick too. Ha. Anyway...

Would I like it if this one was interested? He said it was easy to talk to me. That's a first. Though even if I was a complete bitch and utterly lacking in any social ability, it's pretty hard to be pretentious when you're sitting in a shanty bar being all pretty pink princess and everyone else there could decide to kill you at any moment and get away with it. He was sweet. I'm just gonna call it something nice that happened.

Oh my god...the bar tab was like 50 bucks...for like five of us. I'm pretty sure I said 'Shut up. That's like freeeeee'. Which, considering the audience might have come off as kind of cunty, but dude, it was so cheap. I was actually shocked. The whole night was shocking. I'm not going to get crazy...I've had enough crazy for a minute. And god knows I've still got crazy in the stable...He was just so fucking pleasant. And so so so fucking pretty...Yeah, it's time to move on from that or I'll never get out of this bed. Just so bizarre...Of all the places...and what is it with me and a boy in a baseball cap? What weird ass power do they have?

Oh, right. The Lakes ain't all that. It's like any other country club that looks like your mysteriously wealthy spinster great aunt's house. Like the fabrics were expensive, but there was no real effort made after 1892. It didn't actually smell like old woman, so yay them..but it was sadly, esthetically disappointing. Or maybe not so sadly, because they're a bunch of racist cunts.

Lizzie's coming!! I can't believe I haven't seen her since they left California...Why are we all here now? She's not afraid of the beltway. Is it possible that it's been four years? That's madness. I'm gonna be late.

~~~

Lizzie and I had a good day. I am so glad she's here. Not close enough to be here every minute, but close enough to keep me sane. Painted the kitchen the most amazing orange...Ralph Lauren...Who knew? She and the kids might come back and stay awhile. He is turning into such a piece of shit. Pretty in Alabama ain't universal, Fucker. So now I have to find someone to hang the light and once the table is in, the kitchen will be finished...I sent the waiter the sniff text...I'm weirdly nervous...But nothing ventured...And anyway, one text does not a haunting make. It's

18

not like I'm about to pick up and drive 8 hours to get laid. Though the other voice is like why wouldn't you pursue this a little? You certainly have spent plenty of time pursuing everything not good for you. I hope Jon doesn't think we're having sex tonite...Japan still nags at me. Could we work? In real life? More importantly, will I be upset if I buy a reproduction of the Mackintosh willow chair? Are there even any originals in this country? Is it the design or the pedigree that I really want? Painting the kitchen has made me house nutty.

Oh shit...I might have created a bit of a thing with that boy...I kind of forgot that I asked someone to interview him. Ok well I can't be that person...fuck me again or no job? Not the case, but that's not a good look...dammit. Guess I'm gonna have to throw that one back.

~~~

I am not backsliding. I have completed my first seven days of no Jake contact. There should be a chip for that...But...And there's always a but...I may have been checking his profile and he's so fucking stupid...What he wants is me, but just not me? Me-lite? And even if he did want me me (or does) it's fucked up now, and he will never admit it...Nothing from the waiterboy...I am being super unreasonable in my expectation of communication from something I literally just said I wouldn't pursue...however, no contact from a new potential obsession and no exchange with Japan leads me straight back to Jake. Idle hands.

Tho I do have to consider that maybe he was right...Maybe I wasn't honest about what I want. It doesn't seem that fucking hard, Jake. An amazing lover who is truly on my side and will support me without feeling competitive or jealous and who doesn't want children of his own. I do wonder though if he's relieved at my cold-turkey disengagement...If he cares at all.

Can't stop thinking. I clearly need to be entertained at all times.

~~~

20 pounds need to go. So I'm going to go without alcohol for a while. I need to dry out anyway, and a bottle a day is keeping me fat, in addition to the other implications...So 20 pounds by the wedding. Oh...my baby cousin is getting married. Sucker. I should drop 10 just by losing the wine. Switching back to beer may...nevermind...Alcohol needs to go for a while. Can't be a pig if I'm going to make a habit of fucking youngsters. Gotta take motivation where we can get it.

I bought the Vogue and InStyle. Pre-spring fashion. They both sucked. Sucked. I know better. I hate spring fashion anyway, but objectively these magazines just suck. The three pieces of content they managed to include are garbage, and there's not even anything pretty to look at, which is disappointing. Maybe just don't publish February. It's fucking depressing. I'm feeling a little anxious-even though I just came...And I feel like I could use a drink. That fucker. I really wish I had never met him. Ever. I need to go shopping or something. But I don't want to buy those kids anything. A week. I made it. I wish I could stop the urge for good.

~~~

I should have gone shopping...sobriety breeds contempt...and contempt breeds anxiety...and now, we start the clock over...yes, on both Jake Contact and Alcohol Consumption. Dammit.

~~~

Am I out of energy for the game? I'm kind of sick of men. This weekend I'm going to get my hair done and kick back. If Lafferty wants to come, he can. He doesn't count as men. That window has long since closed. I haven't seen him since the funeral. It's still weird to me that we didn't have sex that night. Maybe because you were still married, genius.

We got pretty close to crossing the line though. I don't remember who played the grown up with morals. Probably him. He also just broke up with another one. Maybe he'll just go full cliche and marry his intern...On a regular day I might wonder if we are meant to be together...Ha. Which is code for I wonder if we're meant to be together. I don't. I'm really exhausted by all of it. I'm tired...Never thought I'd be this tired at 34. Ooooh. Do I wanna watch St. Elmo's? Maybe...I should probably make a girl friend who isn't married or pregnant. Could be my blood sugar.

That little one in my office though is just like a mini-Japan. He said 'whatever' to me today, and I almost punched him in the fucking face. Which is obviously the absolute right vibe for a new workplace.

~~~

Got drunk, sent ridiculous texts and passed out at 10. Cool life. What are you doing?

~~~

Yeah. I'm done. I'm so done. I just looked at a billion men for what? I hate them all anyway. I kind of hope Cutter gets the clap. Is that still a thing? I don't even know which STD that is...Too bad I couldn't have given it to him, though. Why did I see him again? I was making really good progress until...

Until what? Until that other boy who was just a nice thing didn't entertain me? Please. No more, sister. No love. No men. Maybe I'm destined to be alone. Sad and bitter tonight. And no alcohol. Just bile. Angry, disenchanted, and physically repulsed by not trusting my instincts. I am so fucking sad.

Maybe my behavior...no...you know what? Fuck that. I hate that puritanical bullshit. He gets to behave like a fucking prick and then rationalize it by making me into a whore?

That's not what he said. That's the box you think he keeps you in. He doesn't even have enough information to form that opinion.

And I didn't actually fuck him the night we met, so whatever...I think I have an ulcer. This is not the week to quit drinking.

I have considered that I am losing my actual mind.

~~~

Or I'm bored and need to get a hobby. What happened to my fucking plan? Have I let dick make me dumb and complacent? Is this how stoners feel? The fucked up part is that I know this is just healing. Which is more fucking pathetic and annoying than I can stand, and there's nothing to do about it except wait for it to scab over. I should've just stayed married.

Know what else I know? Jake'll come back. And I'll let him. How's that for crazy? Except I'm not.

~~~

Japan is back back, well in contact back. Jon came and put the table together-in exchange for sex because men are fucking charming...It was actually pretty good—easier to enjoy without day to day hate I guess. Anyway, how is it that I feel more like I cheated having an online chat with Japan than having actual sex with my husband? And who am I pretend being faithful to? It's fucking insanity.

Speaking of...I had parent teacher conferences today for the girl. This fucking system...

We're pretty sure she's reading at a much higher level, but she refused to continue answering verbally at grade 6, so that's where we had to cap her official assessment.

I'm sure my face was some combo of murder and bewilderment. I almost choked on my polite composure.

It's reading...why can you not test her *not* verbally??? Like oh I don't know, like in writing for instance.

So we know she's much more advanced, but the rule says they have to talk through it...How fucking ludicrous. I was like yeah, well...when she decides she's done, she's done.

So I'm super glad we chose an award-winning public school system. I almost felt bad for them...They were like we know, but it's the standard. No wonder we're all so fucking stupid. No kid left behind...unless it's a really smart one. Utter bullshit. I was livid.

~~~

Messenger sex (with Japan) now? This is where we are? Is this a thing? It's fucking weird...Not even remotely hot. Some conference in Vegas in the fall. Maybe. I guess we'll play for a bit. Never been to Vegas. It wouldn't hurt to see how we are in real life. As real as Vegas is...Is this really what you're doing? Going back to that crazy? Well whatever...It's like six months away. Will I fall? How fast will I fall? Maybe I won't fall at all. And if it keeps me from the other one...where's the harm? Ha...ohmygod...It's like fucking rebound pinball.

What am I going to wear to Millie's wedding? I'm actually super looking forward to seeing everyone. Ugh. Those children will also require costuming...Which will annoy them, but I am excited for them to get to experience the insanity that I grew up in. Even if it's just a weekend. Maybe we'll go back for Christmas this year.

~~~

Am I about to really be visible on Match? Jackie is all about it. Because she doesn't have to do it. I don't know. It feels sort of desperate. Says the girl having electronic filler sex with what amounts to imaginary lovers.

I'm cool with looking, but participating? I don't know. How do you feel chemistry through a screen? I'd rather play the odds out in real life. Though I don't have a wingman to go out with in real life, so that seems like a go nowhere plan.

What the hell. The photo shoot will give me something to do if nothing else.

~~~

Profile's up. And I have a date?? I feel beyond weird about this. Like a little excited because I'm going out, but also a little like yuck. Meeting him at Ed's, so it's close and if he sucks, I'll at least be able to eat something decent. How late do we think Jon will be?

~~~

Is my life an actual farce? Dude was just whatever. Kinda boring. There was no chemistry. Like kissing myself only duller. Whole lotta drama for very little payoff. Not the date itself, but that fucking dog.

Jon was on time to get them for the first time in the history...So I'm all getting ready and doing my Cher in Moonstruck thing and that dog ate two packs of cigarettes off of the coffee table. I thought I was losing my mind. Searching literally everywhere. Like I just bought them and couldn't find them. I was so annoyed. He's for sure eaten everything, but they don't smell delicious like crayons...They weren't even open...never in the history of his existence. Then Jon called because why wouldn't you need to talk to me two hours after you leave...and as I'm railing about what a complete idiot Diz is, he's all...you know that could kill him right?

Um, no I didn't...I thought he was fucking with me. Turns out not so much.

So I'm googling what to do, and all I could think was that fucking dog will damn well not die on my watch when those kids aren't here. They would never believe that I didn't kill him. Soooo half dozen raw eggs and half a loaf of burnt toast later, I called the emergency vet. Chick's like 'How big is he? Yeah. That's not going to kill him. Have you made him throw up? That's all we're going to do.'

Apparently, hydrogen peroxide is much more efficient than my homemade charcoal concoction. It was legitimately instant. Who knew? Too bad I didn't...before I gave him that egg toast shit to also puke up...stupid internet fuckers. So yeah. I was an hour late after having a full-on heart attack and cleaning up the grossest thing I've seen in a minute...for big fat nothing. Fail. Such a fail. I looked cute though. And good call on Ed's...I do enjoy their chicken wings.

March

Yes, Virginia, the wrath is real. A sofa fell off of the truck in front of Jake today on the highway...Hahahaha. The power will find you. It's not like he died...he didn't even hit it...so maybe half-wrath?? I'm not speaking to him, but that was worth the 30 seconds of returning a text energy and having to restart the contact clock.

I'm making sandwiches and getting the cake for Jackie's shower. How did that happen? I love her, but the cake too? Was I drinking when I said yes? Because of course it has to be a not lame cake, which means I now have to find a not shit bakery here.

Shopping for wedding crap for those children. I'm wearing the cashmere and tasteful sequin skirt number. Maybe if I look like a lady I'll behave.

~~~

The wedding was awesome. I love my family. Danced so much. Even the kids danced like maniacs. I miss dancing. Fucked some friend of her new husband's and was almost certainly still legally drunk when we drove home this morning. Thank god for brunch. I might die if I go to sleep.

~~~

Just finishing up a very quiet kid-free weekend. Not sure where the week went. Doing some intensive learn everything training at work...And it's been sort of quiet on the daily...Japan is deployed. I drunk dialed the boring not as good as kissing myself internet guy. Spent some cash—which I never do, so fuck it. Got Chipotle and now I'm drinking beer in the tub.

AbFab and laundry and dishes. Not a terrible Sunday. I've surely had worse.

Just got off the phone with Japan. I'm not going back there. He's not that magical. He was bitching about his ex-wife poisoning his son against him and now the child won't speak to him, so the only reason for him to come home now is me...I'm not holding my breath. Conceivably, it could be years before I see him.

And sure, most days Jon is worthless, but that shit...that's not what mothers do...unless it's true. He didn't really elaborate other than to say that she's made the kid think that he chose the job specifically so he wouldn't be able to be around. I'm not entirely convinced that that isn't true. But I may be projecting.

I have two months to lose 20 pounds. That Nutrisystem chick lost 20 pounds in two months. I can.

It would help if I stopped eating. Supreme levels of insight today.

I think my mood correlates directly to the presence of the children and the overwhelming sense of resentment I feel building. And he can believe whatever he needs to sleep at night...I might do some fucked up shit, but Jon's not the better parent. They didn't do anything all weekend, so now I get to feel the never-ending mom guilt added pressure to be sure that they're even remotely stimulated in the three hours before bedtime. I don't feel refreshed nor renewed, although I have done a record number of loads of laundry. I'm bored.

April

Husbands don't like me. Husbands who like to control their wives...That's a funny thought...Tho wives who aren't my friends don't like me much either. I think I'm depressed.

I'm for sure a bit foul...The to do list consists of 'pay bills' though, so that's not a big mystery. No Japan this morning. I didn't wait to see if he signed on. I checked email and signed off. He's pissing me off. Which seems unreasonable since he really has no way to control making contact on any kind of schedule. Maybe that's what's pissing me off. Fantastic. 20 pounds. Yogurt, lunch and a shake for dinner. That's it. End of story...And maybe 2 beers. Am I depressed?

~~~

The bad mood didn't last. The little one—has he become my replacement? Dunno but his presence makes me happy. He got the pre-job offer he's been waiting for. So he's out in July. I'm not sure what I'm going to do without him there everyday. And I know he's going to get it because of course he is. My attachment to him is unnatural. Aren't they all...I'm really going to miss him. Like I might cry miss him. Upside...we won't work together anymore. So I won't be shitting where I eat...with a child who's ten years younger than I am.

~~~

I've been talking to myself for a couple of hours. I think it may be time to back away from Japan. Temporarily. Just to see. It's for sure time for his cheap ass to buy a calling card at the very least. He's deployed, so it's Jake Syndrome. Bored and away from the comfort zone. They always like me more when it's a weird circumstance. But he pissed me off on Saturday and then again yesterday and it's not that I'm playing games necessarily, but he's gotta take some initiative. I don't need him like I used to. I am not excited to be the quintessential afterthought and given the logistical circumstances of the current situation, he can buy a fucking calling card. If he's too busy with everything else, then fuck him. I'm preparing for the end of it. He's gotten a lot of mileage out of California. It's about time for some payback. I can obsess (clearly over anyone) for free without continually prostrating my ego...At least until July when the little one exits. Hahahahahahaha. So predictable.

~~~

I'm fat. I'm depressed. And I don't like it here. I need to focus. It's been almost 5 months and all I have to show for it is nail polish and 10 pounds...I am kind of obsessed with it though—it's kind of like hot iridescent coral...I've lost my motivation for the business again. And honestly, it is so hard to get (let alone sustain) momentum by myself. I need a shift. I need some creative work. This is how I got trapped in the Kingdom of Blah (aka marriage) for a decade. Get moving. Do Something. Do fucking anything. Paint your toes. Just find one iota of excitement. One little spark. Stop spending your energy living fucked up romantic scenarios that have no basis is any real happy ending and create the reality that you want to exist. You've come too far to have it all go away. You're too fucking close. I know the down is temporary. I also know that I need an actual on paper business plan. Fuck this place. Am I going to move back to California? What am I wearing?

~~~

The little one wore his glasses today. I almost touched his hair...By Friday I'll be hoping he means it when he says he doesn't want kids. Emotionally attaching like clockwork. It was easier when I just wanted to fuck him. Now I actually like him...

Ugh...that's annoying.

Oh well...I think this would be a good year for a big fucking birthday party...35 and no kids for birthday week. Gig will be here, she says. She doesn't have to fly across the country tho this time, so maybe she'll actually make it. Maybe I'll have a festival...Maybe someone I like might wanna fly in. Maybe I'll ask him now. Am I about to get a keg? Ha...How very hillbilly origin story of me. I'm totally getting a keg.

~~~

And just when you thought the fun had reached its pinnacle...Jon's mommy is coming tonight. She says out of the blue, but there most assuredly was a plan hatched without my knowledge. That fucking boy probably. Judas. The girl doesn't give a shit. I most certainly will be drinking because she's staying with us, of course. Because the grandchildren are here obviously, but also frankly because she likes me better than him. And my house is way better than his stupid ugly ass apartment.

May

Good visit. We actually had fun. Drank like a gallon of wine, which she isn't supposed to do, and laughed and played cards for like six hours. She cleans constantly, which is awesome. She's always like I hope I'm not offending you...which is a lie. She absolutely hopes it offends me, but it doesn't even a little. I fucking love it.

She still won't give me the chicken mole recipe though. She made it while I was at work and then played all coy...Oh, I didn't realize you wanted to help. I just wanted it to be ready for you when you got home.

Ha. Bitch, I've been asking for 10 years. Don't even play.

~~~

Ugh...What the fuck with the East Coast 15? Three pounds of chicken and rice probably didn't help. I drank way more than this in California, so it's not the alcohol. Though I also had way more sex and yoga on the daily, so I guess it's not quite apples to apples...I need to jumpstart this process. Scale's holding strong and the two new pairs of pants I bought aren't quite fitting. And I bought a 12...from Target...A Target size 12. Skirt. A fucking skirt. No fucking way. And when I say not quite fitting-the pants-I mean look bad like sausage. Thighs are repugnant...Gig is coming for the whole summer, so that's good. And they're both going to camp for three weeks.

Just found out I have them for the entire month of June without a break. I mean...I am their actual mother, so it's fine in theory, but their actual father gets to go fly all over...Fair...Do I want that mommy torso makeover surgery? Boobs and tummy tuck should be enough. Inner thigh lipo seems like overkill. Lipo freaks me out...ever since Roseanne said she grew fat back in weird places after hers...I don't need a fucking back goiter. Good thing I like my face or this would be a crazy expensive remodel...The recovery time on that is what? Like a week til I can move? I'm going to buy a blender. Dude...the alcohol has to go. For a week. Surely I can do that for a week...Jesus, I forgot how much fiber 20 grams a day is...it's like a full-time job. I'm actually excited though. Getting back into shape and cleaning out my system...

~~~

They had the good blender at Target. It's like I live there. It weighs a ton, but I'm so happy. We didn't get to Trader Joe's, so I'm trying not to be a freak about my list not being complete. Been up since 530. Brain's flying. So we're back to that. If I'm going to wake up at 530 in a veritable frenzy, I need to make it pay off.

No alcohol, but I ate McDonald's and lost three pounds. First, there is literally no fiber in anything at McDonald's and secondly, why was I at McDonald's at all? Because I was missing two things from my grocery list? That makes less than zero sense. I can't stop eating. I didn't cheat at work today, but I ate three bites of their mac and cheese and some broccoli, and now I'm drinking a beer. Right at 1000 calories tho, so if I don't consume one more thing I'll be good. I really just want to eat.

Japan called and left me the new number...So weird, that. He obviously is able to call now, so why not call when he knows I'm around? Games. Still. I feel like we're pretty close to the actual anniversary. I listened to the message five times. I'm not calling. He doesn't really play with me anymore, so I'm not compelled to seek out boring, old regular people attention. I have an official end of being temporary date at work, so I'll have actual money again.

Do I even want to see him? I would consider Vegas. We could split the difference and meet in Europe. Long way for something so questionable. I don't know if I can play this game for another 3 years.

It's not like I'll stop talking to him, but maybe friends. Maybe I don't even want that anymore.

~~~

Five pounds down and quite gassy from my fiber fest, which is not cute. I didn't call. Had to do my hair. It wasn't even a power play. I just don't feel like performing this morning. I should have just left it curly. And I'm not his first priority, so why should he be mine? I'm tired of initiating and paying, even just for a phone call. Oh, and no more cashmere. I just found like three more sweaters I forgot about. I gotta get ready. If he wants to talk to me today, he can call me.

~~~

So I'm eating my second bowl of kashi (or sad dinner) because I refuse to cheat today. Tho I'm feeling faint. It's my kid weekend, so it's time to settle into boredom. It's ok actually though because I have to clean and set up the Pilates machine. And I so overdid everything last weekend that I could use the two-week detox. It'd also be nice to be at maintenance weight. Took me five months of basically indulging every whim to end up here. My body doesn't think it's supposed to be this heavy anymore, so it should be relatively easy to get back.

So easy in California when I was going out.

Or when I happy.

Even with the turmoil, I was busy and happy and living the life I wanted. Then I lost my drinking buddy and that fuck took away my job. I'm sure it's all some sort of blessing that I can't quite see yet. The little one didn't play with me enough today...Maybe Japan has news. I didn't call. I wonder if he's even noticed. He's probably mad. I hung up on him on Messenger. Whatever. Signing off is way less satisfying than slamming down a phone. Anyway—work was really good today. I had fun??? And soon I'll actually be getting paid real money. And it's all going to be better. I really like them. I wonder if...Can't think. No fat in my system. Totally want a pizza. And a little I wanna call Japan. But I don't feel like I need a beer, so that's good.

~~~

Just ate three egg whites. Dude, less than 60 calories??? I told the girl I would take her for a reuben and s'mores tomorrow. I hate s'mores and I shouldn't eat a reuben, but I can eat half and then more fucking GoLean Crunch. It's 830 in the morning there. Either Japan's sleeping or golfing. I'll wait until 9. That's at least reasonable and if he's golfing today then he's probably already gone. 20 grams of fiber today. Holy shit. Not shitting though. I did get a little dizzy around 4 so I'm going to need to get some nuts or something...Ha. I'm nuts or something.

So he was home. Then work called. Said he had to make a phonecall and would call me back. Got out of the tub, moisturized. made tea. About to light a cigarette and no call yet. I mean, sure maybe he's making coffee or taking a shower, but I am not amused. Again. We were actually having a normal human conversation, so that makes me happy. I'd be happier if I didn't feel nuts because its been almost 20 minutes. And not so much nuts as annoyed. I really don't like being kept waiting.

45 minutes. And that's a wrap on tonite. I'm about 10 seconds from getting off, so if he wants to partake he should probably ring back. I'd rather do it with him, but...Patience. 45 minutes tho? I'm hitting it without him.

Good one. All him. No Jake. That's a first in a long time. Maybe I should just never talk to him again. I swear to god.

~~~

So this morning I'm sorta over it. I feel like I want to have the feelings more than I have the actual feelings...

Here's a weird thing. Last night before he clicked over he said, 'I hope it ain't them.' Not as a joke. As a regular pattern of speech. And I kept thinking about it because it didn't bother me immediately. Like I didn't physically recoil. I wonder tho, if I could really be with someone who uses 'ain't' instead of 'isn't.' Like as an inherent thing...Do I care? Like actually...do I even care? I really liked feeling over the top for him.

Maybe I should just let it die. It would be the best situation. Obsession is no longer clouding my vision. And if he decides it's a thing then he can do the pursuing.

Jackie said something interesting last night. She said that she prays and it helps her (not the interesting part), but she believes the God doesn't necessarily speak directly to you, but that he gives you, or rather provides opportunities on your path everyday and you can take them or ignore them. I feel that. Whether it's God or the Universe. And these are the days...

These are the days of what?

Totally gone...No fat in my system for my brain to use.

Can you have a little ADD? I think I might have a touch. Good creatively. Not so good business wise. Today I get the difference between men's brains and women's. I need a little bit of male tunnel vision. The stage has been set. I know it. And I'm going to have doubts, but what's the fucking problem with that? I don't doubt the fundamental greatness of the plan.

~~~

MICHELLE MARIE

I have to buy pool passes. Hope Gig is really coming. Got 6 weeks to figure it all out. Camp is like 400 a week. The girl doesn't want to go.

~~~

Pilates machine is together. I'm missing a shoulder pad thingy, but I know how to align my fucking shoulders. Totally hating Jon. There is so much shit that he just left here. It makes me nuts. Because of course it's all heavy, so I can't move it.

And now oh my god...The Audrey Hepburn dolls. The level of rage...Apparently, that mother of his just tossed them aside after she let the girl play with them while she was here because I guess when you don't fucking know any better a Barbie is a Barbie. And now I'm missing a shoe and a glove.

Honestly though? Like what was grandma thinking?? Dolls in their original packaging in a box in the basement...I must have what? Fucking forgot to give them to the girl? What if they had been for Christmas? I actually found the coffee cup, which is mind-blowing because it's a millimeter tall. And they all knew that was a fucking boo boo because no one mentioned them at all.

Sometimes it is truly disturbing to realize that everyone thinks I'm as stupid as they are.

1245-no call from Japan. Which is actually OK because now I can hate him too.

It's so gross outside. Hot and humid and disgusting. It was supposed to rain but it hasn't, so it's fucking sickening. I might go watch TV in the basement. Or I might pick up the phone and scream my fucking head off. I think I'm PMS-ing. The boy was supposed to have some movie outing, but it doesn't look like it's going to happen. So we may have to go get a pizza or something. But the basement's still a mess, and no one cares but me. And truth...I barely care. And I only care right now. It'll pass.

740. Got lots of movies. Ate three pieces of pizza. Bad. Still 5 down though, so fuck it. It's finally raining and Japan sucks.

I want to kill everyone and burn this shit to the ground.

~~~

250 AM. Just woke up to a massive skin freak out. Surely pizza cannot work that fast...Or, genius, it could be the downpour that washed all of your hair products into your face.

Whhhhhyyyyy did I check? Why was he online? I was half expecting a text-like caught ya. I almost cried when I was walking back to bed. And not for love lost or any such bullshit, but just because.

It's gotta be PMS. I don't think about Jake unless it's PMS.

8 pounds down at 835. Nice. Ok.

—

It's way later now and I fucking teared up at Ed's eating corned beef. Teared up in the parking garage. Teared up in fucking Banana Republic...Probably though, just because why was I in Banana Republic at all? Some random dude twitched, and it reminded me of Jake.

Gonna be a long life if that's going to continue to be a thing. How am I not past this?

I know the better in the long run bullshit...I just wish it hadn't turned out so badly. Wishing doesn't make it so. I wanted to shop for him today. Why won't that go away?

MICHELLE MARIE

So I guess earlier this morning the tears were for love lost.

~~~

Ugh. I'm so tired of feeling.

I just realized though, because who would I be if I was not be replaying every frame of my life for the past thousand years...I am attracted to people who look like Jake like I used to be attracted to people who look like Japan. And they're not esthetically all that different, so I really haven't made much progress. Creepy.

But I must be hormonal because it's really the only time I get sad about him now. So I'm drinking my last two beers and feeling sorry for myself...and I have to wonder if he's online at 230 in the morning...that kind of means that he's not found anyone. It so doesn't matter. Because I'm not doing it. I'm not acting on the madness. It's such a fucking waste. It's just gotta fade.

I'm like a love junkie.

Reality check: I fell in love twice in three years. Obviously it's not so very hard for me to do. So why all of the fretting? If I fell for two of 10, it really isn't such terrible odds.

So I guess I will wallow in my sad sack bullshit nostalgia for Jake and let it consume me if that's what's gotta happen before it goes away. I loved him. I love him. Can't have him. Don't want him. And that's true Don't want him the way he is now.

There are a lot of boys on Match. And I just got through all of them within 100 miles in like two months. The options are sad.

Like second-rate strip club sad.

~~~

I almost did it today. Holy fuck. I almost lost my mind and grabbed that boy. Twice. Once in the kitchen and once at the desk...Because I watched him take a sip of his coffee and caught a glimpse of his tongue? I almost threw up. I want that a little too much. If he'd just hurry up and get that job I could do it. He's leaving so why not...I'm asking him this weekend. I'll probably get my period Thursday. If I get it tomorrow tho it'll be gone by Friday. That would be too easy. Crazy multiplies exponentially around PMS.

~~~

Got the period last night. So we know what today was—anti-social, wanna crawl in a hole and win some cash in the lottery day. Still five pounds down, and I just ate chicken and mashed potatoes. But it's not even 6 o clock, so I should be good. Had to have it. Wanted a bacon blue cheeseburger. Paid bills.

Strange, strange day. Not as strange as it could have been. I think the omegas are doing their job. I was far less nuts than usual.

Oh, and in my somewhat disconnected state, I may have buried the lead. I touched the little one's stomach—upon invitation, thank you. Casually murmured the appropriate 'impressive' comments. I think I may have been in shock.

I think there's a girl, but he doesn't talk specifically about her. Just kind of hints. There are definitely chicks around. And he fucked some girl in the woods a few weeks ago, so whoever the one I think exists is, she's not the end all be all love of his life. He's a strange boy.

Or I'm obsessively dissecting every minute detail of a regular boy's life. Probably that.

I figure he's ready when he touches me. Though it will never be my stomach because just never. Who does that? Boys who have no body fat and do a lot of fucking core work, that's who.

~~~

I was just having some weird melancholy about what a good wife I was before it all went hard south. What a good couple we were. But...and there is always a but...I don't think I could ever be happy to see him again. Like truly excited to see him for anything other than relieving me of parent duty. And it's really a shame. Because if I felt that, even an ounce, I could stay with him. I wish I missed him. It bothers me that I don't.

It's been five days. Tomorrow will be five days w/o contact from Japan. Good. The aloof thing is not entertaining me any longer.

~~~

I didn't win the lottery. Going to happy hour tomorrow. Leaving the boy and girl at home. I think it's ok. I was babysitting when I was younger than he is.

Guess who's shopping for humans online? Jake. Because of course he is. That's a bad fucking habit. His. And mine, if we're being real. And I sent Japan a nasty email. Because why not call him out, too? Hitting all the high notes.

I'm going to clean. In case of company.

Could I fuck Jake this weekend? Am I strong enough to do that? No. Stupid enough? No. Not tonite. We'll see how tomorrow goes. I might be able to fuck Jake and walk away....I really want to drink, but I can't. Not if I'm drinking tomorrow. It's almost 8 anyway. No more calories. Of any kind. It's not like I could trust that motherfucker to show up even for a booty call...I'd feel like shit if I fucked him. I'm not convinced either way on that right now. It'll keep.

I'd rather see the little one in this bed than some happy hour pick up.

Who knows though? Maybe I'll meet someone cool.

I don't know who I think I'm kidding. If I didn't have my little court jester everyday, I would be texting Jake right now and emailing Japan every minute like a fucking bitch.

~~~

Hair looks pretty. 730. Don't know what I'm wearing...8 pounds down this morning. I totally shouldn't be doing that scale thing every morning. But I need to. I will be so happy when I crack 11. Can't keep up the tiny amounts of food...what to wear?

No baby shower. Jackie went into labor. So I can cancel the cake and save myself a hundred bucks. Guess we're eating turkey and roast beef finger sandwiches for the next six months. I do love pesto.

~~~

I got so fucked up last night...And the hot bartender at Ed's...of course his name is Jake. Why wouldn't it be? Of course he's in a band. Why wouldn't he be? Only thing missing was the red fucking hair. Asked for my number...I drunk dialed the original fucker and hung up...Bad. And because fucking cell phones are from the devil, there is no way now to just miss a call and not know from who. He emailed me hockey pictures. Bad. I wish I could call off today. I feel like shit. I feel really bad. Gonna have to eat bad food bad. It's pouring rain. I got home late. Said I'd be home by 8. Didn't roll in til 10. Another blue-eyed Satan. Bad. Bad. Bad. Puked bad. I made myself, but it wasn't hard.

MICHELLE MARIE

So many Bads.

~~~

Feeling a little psychotic today. Primarily because it only took 24 hours for me to completely unravel. And why do I give a fuck if I wrote down my number correctly for another Jacob? Of course I did, and even if I didn't...so fucking what.

I'm kicking myself for not just inviting the little one over instead of being a pussy. And I'm for sure kicking myself for talking to Cutter at all because I did. And I'm pissed that Japan isn't phoning, even though I don't want to talk to him. And I want to get laid. And I'm feeling completely betrayed by my mind. I'm bored again. And I sort of don't want Jake 2 to call because I was totally into it, and I know myself. I could go to Ed's tonight, but I won't. I'm not going to turn into a fucking bartender groupie. Japan is sleeping. Fucker. I'm going to take a bath. My existence is fucking boring. I'm so bored.

~~~

Drank a bottle of wine and contemplated killing myself for thirty overly dramatic seconds.

Told Jake I was 'getting off the ride.' I'm done. May is a bad month for me.

~~~

The kids have returned and the boy is at Star Wars. I ate enchiladas and corn cake and want to puke. Maybe the name is just bad luck. Anyway, I'm off the Cutter Express I hope. I can't talk to him ever again. No more texts. No more email. No more monitoring.

I met them a year and a day apart—Jake and Japan. That's more freakish than even I can handle. And I have a pretty high tolerance for freak.

I'm feeling the weird compulsion to tell Jake all of it. That needs to fucking pass.

Ha. He said 'what ride?'

I said 'the non-existent us ride.' And thank god I did not pour out all of the deep dark truth of whatever the fuck this heart madness is. I saved a little face. For once.

Cried all weekend.

~~~

It occurs to me that left to my own devices, I could work myself into a complete and total nervous breakdown. So this week, I am going to change my reality.

I'm lonely. So what? Lots of people are lonely. I'll live.

I gained back 6 pounds on my 4 day pity-party bender. But I did manage to pull it together long enough to color my hair because I'm not actually going to give up. Enough is enough...I don't feel strong, but the strength is there somewhere. And this weekend will never have a repeat...Never. Over a boy? Nah.

The fifteen second orgasm is at once magnificent and empty.

~~~

I'm listening to the Jake music. Masochist. I made it through Morphine. Now Elysian Fields...The true test. I might not survive.

Nothing. A little melancholy, but that's more about their vibe and her voice obviously...But no tears. Nothing directly connected to the music. Now it's just mine to listen to. I kind of expected to want to die a little. And I'm not lying. Nothing. Not even a flashback, which considering the debauchery played out to that soundtrack??? Just nothing. And where's the twisted, self-flagellating fun in nothing?

Ughhhhhh. That cocksucker piece of shit who needs to be my ex-husband for real just called to tell me he can't keep those children Monday because he has shit to do. And isn't coming to pick them up until Saturday night because the secret guests who come whenever it's the most inconvenient for me have descended for their surprise holiday visit...Fuck them. Fuck me. Fuck my holiday. Fuck two nights, let alone three. Fuck him. Fuck the other one. Fuck literally everyone. And the most delightful part is that he really could be lying to me, and I would never know. That would be some shit wouldn't it? I suppose though, that's his karma to own. I do however sometimes feel like one of those chicks who buys the conman's bullshit when he tells her he can't share details of his life because he's a spy. Except Jon's job is real, so I just get to be mad.

My horoscope said I woke up today without my rose-colored glasses. Ha.

Those fucking glasses have long since been smashed to bits and scattered in a fucking landfill somewhere in Jersey.

And then...The girl killed my laptop. Explorer is gone. Like gone gone. She put it in the trash as some kind of payback for something I did. I almost put her through the window. Bonus...Also no phone because it's all connected. I'm out of my fucking mind.

~~~

Am I an actual idiot? Did I completely forget what absolute whores bartenders (and Jakes in particular) are? Clearly I've been out of the game too long.

Strippers...that's what they are. And I was totally the limpdick dude with the pile of singles. Oh well...Guess I'll just have to make do with flirting for free liquor. My room looks like an actual tornado tore through it. But the computer and the phone are back. And I fixed that shit all by myself. Literally no idea how. Jon propositioned me again...dude. I'd rather fuck myself...Gonna be a long ass weekend.

~~~

So that happened...the little one. He came out with us. I was like half fake (tho kind of really) belligerent when he said he had to leave. Actually what he said was 'I guess you'll have to play by yourself.' Until about 1030 when he decided not so much and asked if it would be ok to come over. If I had a brain in my head, I would have said no. But the dick's got a mind of its own...

Work's gonna be interesting, but it was so worth it. How bad could it be?

I was borderline demure.

Am I broke for the next month? That seems impossible. Not broke broke, just no shopping trips broke. And the old man is coming, so I won't have to buy food. Do I want a boyfriend? Not the madly in love thing...just like a boyfriend. Do I even know how to do that? I have like two speeds—fuck and marriage. That's not normal.

Ohmygod. Did I break the cursed month of May cycle? I sure did. Just under the wire. Yay me!!

June

So Lizzie just found out that that pig husband has some sex account...Men are depraved...Not just like videos. Some kind of like live sex creepy kink thing. Which wouldn't even matter to mention if he hadn't given some random chick an obscene amount of their money and traveled to fuck her in real life. That'll be the end of life as he knows it for his dumb country ass. She'll be gone in ten minutes. She's eerily not upset. Probably because he's a fucking idiot, and she will enjoy running him into the ground. I almost feel sorry for him. I told her she and the kids could stay here, but I think she's going home to her parents'. So I'm losing my best friend again.

It's looking a little rainy, so I may have to choose a different ensemble. No suede in the rain. Why do I not make rice krispie treats all the time? What was that 7 minutes? And like a dollar...

—

Work was completely normal. We were completely normal. Except for the 20 second kiss in the hall...which was so fucking hot...super light and a little bitey. Then he left. Out of town for the next three days.

Gwen and I went to Ed's. I was glad he wasn't there. My restraint would not have held up very well, and no one needs to know...Jockey was our bartender...Is it weird that a grown man is still going by his childhood nickname? He and Gwen went to college together. He's cute in that regular guy I'm not attracted to way. Other Jake was there. He came over to pay his respects...Never wanna close off the potential tip faucet.

I kinda felt like 'so what...' That's a new one for me. So quickly anyway. I could probably force obsess, but he's got a little kid, so that's a big ol' no thanks...Apparently there is also some baby mama drama because of course there is, bartender in a band...And that, shockingly, is not something I'm down to get mixed up in. Maybe I should be celibate. I'm drunk.

Yeah...Japan told me to call and wasn't home, but someone else female was at home enough to answer his phone. What the fuck is happening? Enough of this. Jesus Mary and Joseph...What am I doing?!! Who the fuck was that? What is this game? Now I'm instantly sober and annoyed. Fuck them all. I am finished. No mas. God knows I have no clue how to pick them. That email just wrote itself. Bye, bitch. I forgot to buy chips.

~~~

Actually woke up in a very good way. Not sad. And not fucking sorry. As I was making the most festive taco dip just now, I was thinking that there's probably a reason why strong women should be alone. I'd rather not wake up again ten years from now in another shitty, boring domestic situation because I fell in love...We're gonna get fucked at tax time. But today I'm happy. And to get so bent out of shape for ordinary humans? Well that's just dumb. I'm too good for that. Too good for Jakes I & II. Too good for Japan. Too much for Jon. Too too...

—

Had a really good day today. Really really good. Makes me wonder why I even concern myself with any of them. I'm not even mad. How can you be mad when a puppy pees on the floor? Well, how can you stay mad? It's probably time to end Japan. Probably way past time... His usefulness has run out. I have friends now and a semi-life, so he's becoming a chore. Never thought that day would come. I'd maybe like to see him just to see if there is/was anything, but realistically I probably won't. I feel like we're forcing something that isn't there. So unless he comes to me...

~~~

I had a sex dream about the little one...which is strange because a) in dreamland we don't usually get past handholding and b) we already had actual sex...so I don't know.

Weird that I never really considered that Japan would be gone for good.

Jon left for Europe, but forgot to call the kids. That is such bullshit. No acceptable excuse for it. I am furious. Like how do you not have a basic parental instinct or even a basic social norm?

I knew him without me was going to be this. Where is the line of protecting them from who he really is and not totally crushing them...Sorry, your dad is very very important in his own fucking head and has zero awareness of anyone or anything else. It's not about you.

I'm sure that wouldn't fuck them up forever...maybe he'll die.

And what about my name? Do I care enough to change it? I'm a little anxious today. PMS and the old man and my brother tomorrow. And truth? Japan too. Why is that making me anxious?

I found the Y3 sneakers I've been coveting forever online. Kinda pricey but seeing as how I don't really do anything in sneakers that would wear them out, I might get them. I am totally getting my period. Gigi is definitely coming. I'm a little too excited about that. And she bought her ticket, so no California repeat. Once I have someone here to hang out with on the regular...I'll be so over them. Will they always be able to reel me back in? Probably for a while, but maybe I won't make it so easy for them. The boy only wants to go to camp for two weeks, and it's 800 bucks. So I guess Jon and I will split it. Maybe I can keep the house in an adult human state of clean with her here too. Jake hid his profile. Maybe he found The One, the new for now one. Maybe I need to never get my period. He was inactive for 3 days and now he's hidden. That really is the perfect device for him. So why wouldn't I just text him? Yes I did. I'm just amusing myself. Because the actual shit I need to be doing, like cleaning and shopping for company, holds no dramatic appeal.

I just did that math that one does in order to procrastinate, and I know though that cleaning will only take like 3 hours, so why would I start now? Annnndddd...I survived my first 6 months here without killing myself or anyone else...Nice.

Now I am a slave to the flashing light and lack thereof on the cell. I just got totally psyched over the flashing red...my neighbor. When did I give her my number? I know I'm getting my period because I'm totally faltering on my decisions(s). All of a sudden, like in the span of a couple of hours, I'm feeling weak. And I haven't cleaned a thing. Don't feel like it. Feel like frenzied shit. Want to be wanted by someone I want. Want to be in a house on the water. With my company and my children and a forever love. Dude, what the fuck? There are golf courses out the ass here...Tho, if one thing has to give, I'm ok with it being love. So long as I have friends. So I guess I'm not faltering. Just wishing it wasn't so difficult. It's probably for the best...Japan really does have a small penis. And so begins the drinking. Saturday self-medication ritual. So pleasant. Vacuum, clean the bathrooms, wash some shit and I'm done.

7 am. That's when I'll clean. Or I could start now, but I don't really care. There's a theme.

I just designed my house. Like all of it. In detail. What is my obsession with sunken rooms? Well, whatever...but I'm sure that it will be delightful for the architect I hand the sketches to. Yes, that is college-ruled paper. No, I don't know math or load bearing wall rules. Ignore all the dick talk on the neighboring pages.

Am I about to buy a massage chair?

~~~

Ugh...If I build here, am I going to have to cowtow to a fucking association?

Japan got all pissy...started with Here you go again. I've been traveling for five days and this is what I see when I get back blah blah blah. If that's what you want, fine. Nothing to apologize for.

Fuck him. I answered K.

I mean, I kind of forgot that I sent that email. I send so many. I knew I was pushing. I pushed on purpose. If it's going to be done, then it's done. I have real people to entertain.

~~~

Jon's car got broken into. So he's not dead, but dude...Don't be a cunt and bad shit won't happen to you. I apologized to Japan when I got home from work. Because I am stupid, but also because I totally overreacted. Though, if someone had mentioned he had a house sitter...I'm not bringing up anything anymore. If we could see each other, then I'd either be cured or convinced. I'm done wishing he would 'come to his senses'.

I'm the one who needs some fucking sense. Perpetually.

~~~

Really? Am I about to do some recon on a political wunderkind? This is what happens when I actually open a newspaper instead of just letting them pile up. Surely though, in order to get that high in the government by my age, you can't have any kind of outside life. Interesting. I'm thinking about buying a Land Rover. I'm cooking spaghetti and drinking white zin. It's gross, but it's my father's attempt at hanging with me. I look really good today. I'm excited to have seemingly found a home and I'm comfortable here, so I can proceed with the empire. Light stalking of conservative politicos aside, love is on hold now.

~~~

And of course...the irony...now you wanna have phone sex? After I came. I didn't respond. I'm going to test drive Rovers this weekend. And dude, if you want me back the sex had better be good. And real. Lizzie comes tomorrow. The little one, who my brother says I shouldn't have to ask out no matter how young he is...I may have left a piece out...today I was looking at his face. Like at it for real. The eyes, the lashes, the freckles, the chin...is this going to be a thing?

~~~

Blue book on the Rover is 15. I should probably wait until I have an actual paycheck.

And later...Got the 'you online?' email from Japan. It's nice I guess, but what difference does it make if it's not in person cause this is some new Match boyfriend level fake bullshit.

Lizzie's here hanging out with us. She met some guy in Scotland playing some online game and they're like in love. Like she's moving there. What the fuck? And Jon's fat brother just called and invited himself to visit next weekend. I said we were out of town. And I'm really drunk or I would be cataloguing my new and exciting email from my potential business partner. Which is far more important than men who annoy me.

~~~

Company is about to roll. Put my bro on the plane yesterday. Old man is leaving today.

So I did get my period. And not saying they're related, but when my father mentioned that by the way, the guy he wants me to call for business advice said, 'don't do it.'

Bless his heart, tryin' to help but...Holy fuck dude, really?

Then as he does when he senses danger, he tried to soften. 'Maybe it would be a good idea to talk to someone with a different perspective.' I was like yeah, no. I'm not calling him.

The only different perspective I want is a different approach on the how. 'Don't do it' is just a fucking non-starter. What's the point? I mean maybe I will fail, but why would I start with a fucking naysayer who I know is a naysayer before I even pick up the phone? I already know all of the cons. I got them from actual experts. I don't need to hear them from some bloated old fuckstick whose prime has passed. No room for naysayers. Especially naysayers who weren't at the top of their game even in their time. Fucking old men...They think they're all so wise just because they've survived a few decades more.

Like I should be honored to drop to my knees and suck from your old shriveled dick of knowledge just because you're what? Still alive?

So, no friend...I won't be calling.

~~~

Finally alone. Of course I'll be nutty bored in a couple of days. As a bonus parting gift yesterday, the old man also left the front door open while he was loading his car and Diz got hit by a bus...A fucking bus. I don't think he's ever even seen a bus. He's fine...a thousand dollars later. Which I did not even pretend to attempt to offer to pay for. I was like you took him to the wrong vet without even calling me...I wasn't nice. And my thank you was snarky and not the least bit sincere. Guess now I get to teach him about traffic. And on goes the fucking list of shit I get to do.

—

Watching the dog pace around the room. And pant. And fart. I cannot imagine that's a good thing. There weren't any notes on what to watch for. Hopefully he sleeps soon.

~~~

Is there anything more visually confusing than a dog shitting blood? Which is hopefully over now that I had the medicine changed. But fuck me really? Gushing blood out of his ass? Maybe you could have sent a list of potential side effects for a grand. I have never seen anything like it. What a fucking week.

I am in desperate need of some bigger thinkers in my world.

Watched Flashdance yesterday. I fucking love Irene Cara. Fame and Flashdance? Love her. Anyway, I'm going to find a dance class. Or not today in this place I'm not because they're all for children. And this girl's recital days are over.

So in lieu of any productive way to lift my spirit, I spent an hour digging for intel on a government man who is not just a suit, but an uber-suit. I don't really find myself having a use for many men who wear suits. And a white Southern Republican...That's not just a suit. That's an uber-suit. Though if he has a wife, I sure as shit couldn't find her. That's the next husband. If I'm gonna have one. Fuck the plebes.

Oh...maybe he's gay. Tho, that would have to be the most beyond extreme down-low situation. GOP ain't big fans.

~~~

Best Sunday in a long long time. Magazines and music. Had a bath. Finally made contact with the designer dude for my logo. Dog cured of his intestinal issues. Got the boy a haircut. Found a new favorite shopping plaza. Actually did some creative work. Bought a killer pooper scooper. Found some new hair products. Overall great day. A few splurges, but not really. Great ending to a bizarre week. Although who is that excited about a pooper scooper? Who am I becoming?

Enter Mr. Cutter. Interesting. But not really. Play for a couple of minutes maybe, but then I'm done.

Or I'm done now. He's on the other side of the country where it's safe to engage me. So he's bored. Not getting sucked back in.

He said something weird and vague about my language being erotic. Erratic is more like it. Regardless, he knows it will make me think, which will give him enough of a crack to re-infiltrate. And of course it worked, because now I'm wondering if that's part of the whole whore-box thing. Not that I care necessarily that he thinks of me in any specific way. I was just talking, and what's the point of explaining anyway?

The butterflies are still there when I think about kissing him. Ughhhhhhhhh

~~~

I shouldn't even waste the ink to say that Cutter didn't call back. I'm not surprised. I'm not even disappointed. It's better. I'm a little sleepy today. And sore because I jumped around my room for like three hours. Truthfully, I would have liked to have phone sex because it's hot listening to him get off. And Japan is currently out of frame. And dammit. Yesterday I was so ok with it. I was really great. Then Jake. Again. Fucker. Just shit or get off the pot. Never thought I'd want a Sunday back. Oh well. No do-overs. Cold turkey. Also, no more tuna subs either because that's been happening...maybe I have an iodine deficiency. For real tho...I'm finished stroking egos.

If I'm going to fret, the payoff needs to be better. Time to expand the circle. Can I just also say never underestimate the power of the fucking hair. Wore it down today. Such simple creatures. I really really wanna kiss Jake. Wish that would go the fuck away.

~~~

I need to detox my whole existence. Not just this +13 pound body. Like a proper cleansing, some exorcist level shit. Text and an email and then just didn't call. Why do I think he'll ever be any different? Just gonna put all my energy into the work I get paid to do...Let's go earn our money.

Kissed the little one today in the office. I don't know what I'm doing. He's leaving. And it's hot. And I'm not his boss, so fuck it.

~~~

Tentative plans to see Jake the week after next. I'm not counting on it even though he brought it up. Then he told me they cut his orders for Iraq. By mistake. Two weeks ago. Is that what happened? Did it scare him enough to stop fucking around? My baby in Iraq...No.

My baby? What is that? No. Nope. No.

~~~

I'm not going to want to cook. I wonder if he's going to sleep over. Surely. I'm trying not to get carried away, so I'm going to focus on what I might wear. I mean, I'm not feeling carried away. Feeling almost casual. Didn't text him all day and I'm not drinking, so that will not factor in. Make no mistake though, it's shakes and green tea for the next ten days. He hasn't signed on to that devil site for three days...

~~~

Might have to be rooibos today. Out of green. Hope is the worst drug. The little one expressed interest in happy hour yesterday in mixed company. I was immediately and irrationally pissed. I'm not sure why though. Can I deal with 3-5 cups of green tea a day as like a way of life? That's a lot of tea. I'll stop on the way home from work. Coffee is keeping me fat. Was I mad that he wasn't just telling me he wanted to come over? Or was I mad that he was inviting people into our secret? Or was I mad just because he wanted to go out with everyone? Something triggered the rage. I came down from it pretty quickly, but it was there. That's not good.

~~~

It wasn't a mistake. He's going to Iraq. And I know only because he posted it publicly on Match.

~~~

And now Jon is on the phone and he's drunk. I'm trying to focus...blah blah blah...about his trip. I might kill him.

So I'm WASTED and the sun's still up. And I'm not sure what to do about Cutter and Iraq, mostly because I know, but I'm not really supposed to know. Because he didn't tell me.

Part of me is just like fuck it. He wants a new piece or sever. before he leaves? That has never had less to do with me. I just wish I didn't know.

720 and drunk as a skunk...No more wine.

Two glasses did me in. Two big ones though. Which is really just alcoholic math for a bottle.

Here's what...Fuck him.

If he wants to take up the cross and find a new chick before he goes, let him. I wish I didn't love him. I wish I wasn't speaking to him. I wish any number of things. Here's the other thing...

What if the worst...

Nope. Got nothing to do with me. Not my drama. Not my war. Not about me. God, I hate how uncontrollably compulsive I am. Whatever. I looked. I have to own what I found...He's using Iraq to score. Do I want this person? Like actually? It's just a ploy to get laid. What do I care? I'm a big fan of fuck whoever you wanna fuck...This though, I think it's a little sick...Am I a hypocrite? 730

~~~

I got soooo paid! Yay! I am 3 pounds lighter. And sore. Yoga. Am ambivalent about Cutter. I might be a little hurt that he'd rather spend his last weeks with a stranger or strangers, but it's his life. It's not about me. I don't really need to have a boyfriend at war anyway. So he's doing me a favor.

Truth though...he wants me in, I'm in. Like that was a question. No one believed that blasé whatever happens happens shit...But he has to decide. I'm not begging to be in this storm. I would like nothing more than for him to realize that we are the real thing, but that's not my call. And frankly, I'm not spending the next year writing and sending gifts and waiting so that he can decide to pull a Christmas at the end. So the choice is his. I will not be manipulated again.

~~~

Oh ye of little resolve...

But I love him...yeah, that was in full whine.

The saddest part. The most pathetic part...I love both of them. And how is that possible? Do I just love them both forever or maybe just until I love someone new? I'm going to the store.

He's out getting fucked up. I just saw a hot firefighter. Which made me smile. Bought a bunch of food I'm not going to eat. I will probably cry tonite. But I'm not going to give in and profess my love. No matter how much I drink. As I was pulling in I thought about fucking the little one again.

Jake will just have to be the one who got away.

No. I fucking hate the implication of that statement. Like he's such a fucking prize.

The one I wanted so badly I might have had another baby maybe...Really? Yeah. That's how fucked up it is. And he knows it...I've gotta keep my shit in check. No contact. Let him do whatever he needs to do.

A baby? Hahahahahaha. Fuck that. I just caught my pretty self in the mirror. A baby...Fuck him.

~~~

We're back to cell flashing means Jon. These past couple of weeks have actually been nice with him being gone. And I wouldn't really care if the kids were always here...today. Next weekend will be different.

MICHELLE MARIE

Montessori is 10 grand. So now I'm considering the arts magnet. I'm not paying ten thousand dollars for 1st grade. They're both going into lessons this year, though, so I could divert the tuition to that. I guess the tech school is also a good place for her. She's too smart and good at everything. And I'm pretty sure she has figured out how to launch a nuke from the laptop so maybe a tech focus is a good fit. Who the fuck knows. Gotta find her thing. Gotta focus that genius before she starts killing people and burying them in the crawlspace. Jon will have to pay for activities. Fuck him. Never being able to count on him to be here. I'm keeping the car.

~~~

No word from Jake. Cried a little. But it's done. Said goodbye to him last night. He's too much work. Now I need a new plan for this weekend. In a month I won't even be able to text him. Thank Christ. And today I am very glad that I didn't bring up the post. Let someone else have the mindfuck.

Little bits of tears. I'm crushed. Not surprised, but crushed. Again. Only have one beer with which to numb out. I'm not feeling super philosophical today. Bitter and angry though for sure. This is no one else's fault though. I'm the one who fell. I'm the one who refused to let go. They were just being themselves. Their pig ass selfish bullshit selves. And I kept coming back. I hope I learned something. Like I hope I won't be the exactly the same the next time.

I got more beer cause it's more fun and way faster than Prozac. And now I'm pooping. Had a few bites of mac & cheese, which is basically all those fucking children will eat now.

So the boy just gouged his head on a tailpipe?? and was pouring blood in the parking lot. Jon didn't pick up his phone. Screaming voicemail and frantic escalating to murderous texts eventually moved him to action. Said anything on the head or face always looks worse than it is blah blah bleeds more, and he'll come up tomorrow???

What kind of father doesn't pick up the phone when his son has a gushing head wound? The level of hate...

Though it did in fact look worse than it was once I cleaned it. But that's not even close to being the point.

I am plotting many deaths.

I can't believe I was up here drinking beer and planning to fuck whoever and my son was bleeding all over the pavement.

Also though, what the fuck? There's grass literally everywhere here. Football on the pavement? It's not Detroit.

~~~

Slept on the floor so I could wake him up and check pupils and responsiveness intermittently. I'm sure that was a great night's rest for him. The head looks bad. But he doesn't want to stay home. And he seems ok. I am raging with disgust and feel like shit. Hangover much? So that was my night... Now I'm waiting for Jon to show up. And not a warm nor fuzzy thought about any of the assholes today. Oh, and my birthday hootenanny plan is fucked.

~~~

Jon has a youngster named Melissa (which makes 3 in my orbit now??) who calls him...wait for it...Sweetness. Barf. Though that explains where he fucking was yesterday. Sweetness though? Fucking really? She doesn't really strike me as a Morrissey fan though, so maybe it's just what all the kids are saying...and me. Cause that for sure what I used to call Jake. I wonder if he'll tell MissyLouWho that he fucked his wife. Wasn't horrible. Sterile and something to do.

Sweetness. That's what I get for nosing through his texts. Fucking gross.

—

And at 1017 pm...'you alright love?' Really, Jake? He's fucking good. And I'm fucking easy. I waited and debated for ten minutes before responding 'I'm fine.' Then I sent him 'Saturday. 7' and the address. Cause I'm done. He shows, he shows. He doesn't, fuck him. I'm painting the living room on Saturday. Love though? Sweetness and Love in one day? This is ridiculous...

My dad asked me once 'Did you ever think it might be you?'

Ha...Of this I'm certain.

~~~

Of all that is holy in this world...It is totally back up there, the post...Iraq for a year. That crazy motherfucker. Penpals??? He's insane. Something to look forward to??? Crazier than I ever even imagined. God almighty...

Yeah, I need him to be where I can't text or call. I'm not going to cave. This is his choice. I don't want a fake fucking boyfriend, let alone one in Iraq.

I know this is one of the weirder considerations...but is it possible that he doesn't know me well enough to know that I would see that because I am absolutely keeping tabs on his every move? Have I given him too much credit? Could he legitimately not think I know?

It's like a fucking chess game. That I'm playing against myself though pretty much.

Why can't anyone just be honest?

Though, I really only want the honesty I want.

~~~

Calmer today. Going to try to keep the frenzy at bay. Go to the girl's music program (Jon isn't because he's a douche), go to work. Jackie is bringing that baby over tomorrow. And thus begins my busy weekend.

I was honest. Not like 100% extra shit that doesn't matter honest because I'm not an idiot. But honest in a vacuum about my feelings.

I could pretend that I was just providing him context because I didn't want him to show up under false pretenses. But really, I just basically guaranteed that he won't show up at all.

'I love you. And all who come after are suspect. Because beware the chick who wants to be a war girlfriend.'

I know he has trust issues. And I know whether he talks to me ever again or not, he'll internalize that. There's some deep dark thing that will keep him from ever being happy.

It's so twisted...

A. I want him to show. B. I have little faith that it will happen. C. I make an overtly offensive defensive move to keep him away.

I'm sure a shrink would have a field day with that.

Maybe I'm more interested in playing the game than I'd like to admit. Or winning it.

Either way, I'm fairly certain I'm not going to see Jake again. And it's not quite ok right this minute, but I'll get there. I've already died a few Jacob Cutter deaths, so it's not like I don't know how it works.

~~~

And then just guess what? Or should I say who? Japan. Like fucking clockwork. I swear to god they're in cahoots. Tagging you in. This week she's your problem...

It's nice I guess that he thinks of me, but I don't have anything left. Yep and Jon is going to be late. Shocking. I'm going to tape the living room.

~~~

Living room looks amazing. And I might have fucked the cable guy. Which is weird and porny, but they're rarely hot...so whatever.

He just straight up didn't call. Now I have a Sunday to myself. If I wasn't so physically tired, I would probably feel more...I didn't ask because I need to stop giving him the satisfaction, but I slow boil hate him. I'm going to take a bath.

—

Cried all the way to pick up the kids and yelled and was shitty all the way home with the rage music at top volume.

July

It's the little one's last day. I'm really sad. We're taking him out later. That makes me nervous.

I'm not stable enough to deal with this. It's not like I'm in love with him, but it was a thing. A happy, playful thing. I'm going to miss him. I hope I don't cry.

~~~

I didn't cry. I put on my social face and executed my part to perfection. We kissed in the garage, but I didn't invite him and he didn't ask. And off he went. And that was that. I expected to feel emptier. Ha. There's always tomorrow.

~~~

Gigi is here!! Bought a new TV. Kids are only going to one week of camp now. Dreamed about Jake. Feels weird without the little one. Not sure what I'm going to do all day now...work maybe. Gig thinks Japan looks like a nice guy. Uh-huh. It is totally disgusting outside. I almost stepped on a frog. Toad. Whatever. Fucking gross.

Oh. And how did I not realize that she's dating Trina's old distraction? The painter. That will be a fun conversation to hopefully never have with either of them. What kind of small world magic dick shit is this? My cousin and my best friend since high school? They already hate each other...I'm not quite sure of the timeline, but I don't think there's any overlap. These people...

It's a city for christ sake. How?? I know how...so he's probably got like four more...at least.

Japan is about to embark on some secret detail. I should probably dispense with military men.

~~~

I am full blown obsessed with Frand Ferdinand...Can I never just like anything??? Zero middle ground. At least there's still one decent radio station here. You'd think with the 8000 colleges that one of them would have a station. I'm like that old person now...In my day...but like for real an old person...I asked that band child in my office today...what's that dingydingydingy part on Take Me Out...and I swear to god like in slow motion for emphasis, he brushed that swoopy hair out of his eyes and said...ummm you mean the guitar? Smug little bastard...He's cute tho.

Oh...and Gig is in love with him. Like moving in together, coo on the phone, can't stop smiling in love...fuck me. She knows about Trina. Well, that it was a thing once anyway...I feel like he did that 70% honest thing tho...Although Trina is a psycho, so who knows what the truth is. Jake is in Colorado—training. I cried again this morning.

~~~

Fuck, I hate summer. This place might be actual hell. It's so fucking humid. Did I just have a fight about Canon's superiority over Nikon with a dude for like an hour? He was committed too. Special Agent Lucky O'Charms. It's really Donovan O'Flannigan or Milligan O'Reilly or some couldn't be more Irish name, which is the same thing in my head. Not a redhead, but he's a douchebag. He thought he was being all sorts of edgy when he asked if we'd have a threesome after we told him we were cousins...

Dude nah...We haven't done that since we were little...

Can we talk about the deer? Like I don't already hate them enough, not the sweet little ones with the spots, obviously, but the adult deer here are fucking belligerent. Gig and I decided if we walked five miles a day it would counteract all of the drinking, and every morning we see them. They just stand in the path and look at us. They don't spook and run. It's fucking scary. And they're huge. I'm convinced they're all rabid. Am I about to become a hunter?

More frogs too...It's an omen.

~~~

Are frogs one of the actual signs of the apocalypse? Are locusts next? I don't think this is normal...I should find a bible. It's seriously disturbing. Not just a couple. They are everywhere. Can't even open the front door without making sure they're not right there waiting to jump into the house. I don't do well with infestations. If this house wasn't made of cardboard I would light the whole fucking yard on fire...At least they're not falling out of the trees. That would send me over the edge.

On a not frog trauma note, the new theatre boy we hired gave me the entire box set of Buffy to watch. How have I never seen it?

So that's healthy...frogs and vampires and alcohol and fucktard boys who wanna watch me fuck my cousin...Yay summer. What atrocities did I commit in my last life? The world has gone mad. It's fucking surreal. Oh...I got promoted again.

~~~

It's like I'm new...major party foul...where is my bag, my phone, my keys freakout. Except they weren't right next to me like they usually are. So panicked that I just flew out of the house and one of those little fuckers hopped right in the door. I screamed and punted him back out. I hope I killed him. Probably not...He probably just called in reinforcements. My bag was on the post. Thank god we live here I guess 'cause it was out there all night. We should probably walk the ten feet to Ed's from now on...We won't because why be responsible adults when we can be lazy degenerates?

Ughhhh. This is McDonald's bad. Now we're gonna fight over who goes. If they delivered even just on weekend mornings they'd make so much more fucking money...Like they need more money.

Oh my god. Is this place built on a hellmouth?

August

Soooo, class...here's the first reason we don't blow boys in cars—even super cute boys who drive super cute cars...cause if even a microscopic droplet of cum splashes into your eye, you can flush that shit with water for an hour and it'll still swell shut for two days and you won't be able to tell anyone why. You'll find yourself smiling like an asshole as you say lots of inane shit like 'It is super weird. I'm not exactly sure. Dust maybe? Spider bite? Allergies?'

And that is an utterly charming predicament for a mother of two who is also playing the role of a professional boss of people.

So much for eyelashes and reflexes.

The other reason we don't commit said sex act? That cute boy can't separate that hooker from the person they asked out earlier in the evening...I won't be holding my breath for that call. Hot though. And a civilian. Am I turning a corner?

Gig is leaving. The love pull is apparently too much. I think she just doesn't trust him. The fact that she made it this long is amazing. I knew she was going to leave last week after the Trina fight happened. He was a little sketchy about when he saw her last. It's probably for the best that she goes back. Trina doesn't like to lose, and she's a raging whore romantic who hates her husband and has convinced herself that this one's her soulmate so...speaking of thoroughly deluding and distracting oneself, Japan has surfaced, literally...And it seems that he is going to Vegas.

And Thank Old Testament God...this toad frog odyssey is not a normal occurrence. I have asked everyone in this neighborhood. And nope...just my lucky fucking year.

MICHELLE MARIE

~~~

Just took Gig to the airport. So that's going to make for some idle time. I have like a season of Buffy left which may or may not keep me out of trouble...I feel sorta sad, but two grownups in a house when they're not fucking is a lot...complicated by the Boy With The Magic Penis/Gigi/Trina triangle, which is not my business, but kind of is because they're both my people...and Gig is going to win, but is he worth it? Who knows? That svengali dick is powerful. Empty house. I'm kind of in love with it.

Hell yeah!

That was my answer for Vegas. Guess we're going to Vegas in October. And we'll see if it's there or not. I'm closing chapters. The little one is gone, so whatever that was or wasn't is closed. Jake is closed. Well, bookmarked at least. And now Japan? He remains open until October. Then we decide.

~~~

So Cutter did what Cutter does when he senses his hold loosening. Called and apologized. And asked me to write to him. If I could capture the intensity of the pursing of my lips and rolling of my eyes even just writing the words.

I will do it of course.

And I will fully rationalize it as my duty as a patriot to support the only troop I actually know.

I'm a fucking idiot.

I'm still going to Vegas.

~~~

Jon's introducing the new girlfriend to the kids today.

Cryptic letter en route from Jake—like I sent you a letter. Fascinating.

I'm already expecting way too much from it. He's giving me just enough to cement my commitment. But really, unless he asks me to marry him—I owe him nothing. Less actually.

Wait. Is that what I think?

Do I think he's going to profess his undying love for me?

That he's going to promise himself to me right before he goes into a war zone?

And even if that were to be the case, that any such declaration would mean anything?

—

The new girlfriend's a hit. Life is uncommonly fair. He's a fuck-off for a decade, then he gets everything his way...Super fair.

~~~

Last night Jake asked me why I still speak to him. I said I shouldn't be but blahblahblah love conquers all.

We had a good talk about what's important and not being cunts to each other, but it wasn't that much different than the 8 million conversations we've had before..except this time there's a war (and a fucking blog).

It was all very well-scripted.

Never had anyone who challenges him or was so passionate. The next year will put his craziness in perspective. Allow him to realize what's important...Maybe we could use this as a fresh start of sorts. He's a walking disaster area. The next year is what he needs to get over himself.

Uh huh...I ignored all of that and just straight up said are you done with the Internet bullshit? Because I'm not dealing with that nonsense.

I can't let myself trust him completely. And I'm not making the the investment I made before. And if it's going to work on any level, he has to be honest. He said he was being honest.

Honest...That's an elastic word though isn't it?

Somewhere hidden in the midst of all of that though, was this little gem: 'I think the next twelve months will bode well for you.'

Like what the actual fuck does that mean? I obviously know exactly what he means, and I'm more than a little annoyed.

He really believes that he's the fucking prize.

I didn't flip out though. I kind of chalked it up to stream of consciousness because I have to in order to be all in, don't I?

But whatever...Big picture it is still war, and I feel like that trumps the bullshit.

Of course you do because how else could you justify completely abandoning everything you already know to be true?

This should go swimmingly. Detachment is so my thing.

~~~

Trina told me I'm a fucking idiot, and I've set myself up to effectively not be interested in meeting anyone I could actually be with. Which

I readily admit is true, and add in Japan and I've doubled down on it...but of all the people to offer relationship advice? Bitch, please...He gets leave in six months. I'd be lying though if I said I wasn't reconsidering Vegas. Except that there are no guarantees that whatever this is will even hold together til then. We are talking about Jake. He's got very little credibility in this arena. She had the baby. Going to visit weekend after next. Hope it looks like her husband.

September

You know that feeling...the one where in spite of your mind screaming SUCKER you believe all of the words...Never felt the emotional pull. Was afraid of it. How powerful he feels when we're together...followed up with an elaborate story that got me off like four times...

That feeling that you cannot control the depth of whatever this addiction is...is it love? I don't know. I call it that. It makes me feel out of control and vulnerable and crazy. And dumb. So dumb. Unrecognizably dumb.

Oh and earlier, the boy told me that I shouldn't date anyone because I have kids.

I told him that he should stop eating sugar because diabetes runs in Jon's family because God hates them.

~~~

Two chicks. Two messages. On the blog. He's not even on the fucking plane to Kuwait yet. Game on, motherfucker. Now we'll see. I want to fucking scream.

And now that I've calmed down and done all of the recon that I require...because everyone has a fucking blog because they're all so very fascinating...got four years on his sister and his brother's fucking hot.

I'm not sure I can handle the madness. Or I'm about to go full on into it.

We all know what you're gonna do.

~~~

Letter came.

Here's the letter. Chat later babe. Jake.

Japan, however, sent a nearly proper email...I'm going to Vegas. I don't owe anyone anything. And I'm not feeling so gracious.

I got a raise.

~~~

There was/is a girlfriend...In his office. And she's something because she has physical custody of all of his music. While he was in the air, she took it upon herself to introduce herself to the family. He won't like that even a little bit. I do so enjoy a virtual guestbook, where I can strategically indulge my instant gratification jones and rage monster while posting a tasteful and anonymous love message. I have been off my nut for two days. Got really drunk and puked. Pretty.

~~~

Hahahahahahaha. She, this dishrag of a girl, called me out—wait for it—in her online journal??? Is that an actual thing? Who are these people? Why the fuck would you let the world in on your private crazy? She doesn't even know who I am, like as a person not 'she doesn't know who she's messing with.' Moreover, she has no idea who he is...but girlfriend's gonna find out.

In response to my you are my heart or whatever sappy bullshit I posted...She said ON HER ONLINE JOURNAL...I'm not that nice, and you will regret it.

What.the.fuck.

I'm sure he told her my entry was a joke or feigned complete ignorance as to who would have written such a thing. But if she's even a little smart, she won't believe him. She means nothing to me. I'm not sure right now he does either.

I like my position. And I am thoroughly entertained.

Am I really this cool about this? I think I am. No more looking at blogs though. Much. I don't want to know anything else. He will have to buy me something pretty for doing his dirty work. I feel nuts right now. Not hurt nuts. Just nuts.

Dude tho, for real...She fucking called me out. Well, inasmuch as she captured her innermost thoughts about me...FOR THE WORLD. That's pretty funny. Silly, silly rabbit.

~~~

My stomach is undone. Too much drama. Already. Not that I'm not enjoying it a little. But fuck. Emotional eating is my thing. Ooooh. Do I think I can ride this unable to eat wave right back to my size 5 ass?

~~~

I hate her. Did that need saying? Not because he was with her. He can't really be with anyone...But I mean she introduced herself as his girlfriend to his fucking sister...on his sister's blog (of course)...If you don't know that the family is off limits then you don't get him even a little. I'm done now. I will stop entertaining thoughts of bringing that girl's world to a thunderous halt. The tone in her journal is bad. Welcome to Jake's Big World of Fuck.

The next year will bode well for me. Jesus Christ. Closed this chapter. Opened it right the fuck back up. And it's making me sick. Sick. No control over him. No control over war. No control over anything but myself—and that hold is tenuous at best. Get a grip, sister.

Jacob Cutter is not the prize.

I should tattoo that on my forehead backwards.

~~~

Seriously? I've been drinking since one. Six o'clock now and I'm about to go out for happy hour and dinner...My stomach is out of control.

Am I afraid he'll die?

Truth? I'm more afraid he'll live and fuck me over again. And all of this will have been just another entry of me being stupid and believing in what? What I can see is the truth? Dude, it is just so far buried that I'm not sure it matters.

Think I'm gonna get laid tonite. Enough soul battling.

~~~

Hooked up last night and didn't even think about you. Ha. Didn't think about *you*? Apparently on some level I did.

Lucky O' Charms didn't really wanna play ball my way. Shouldn't hold yourself out as a freak if you're really just vanilla. Am I losing my touch?

Sent him the I know about her email. Twelve hours of alcohol is not going to be a plan if I'm going to live.

He said 'What the hell are you talking about?'

Did I miss the mark on his level of intelligence? I'm not really in the mood to play, so I just said End it.

I'm not going to let him make me the psycho who can't appreciate that his current reality is a holding pen in Kuwait.

~~~

Made my political appearance at the company pool party yesterday. Like needles in my eyes. I hate picnics.

Dude, Lucky Charms is the same personality. Or I wouldn't be attracted. I think it's way past time to exercise a little self-control. I'm doing nothing. Am I depressed? How much work is this meant to be? Why am I not building my own thing? I want to hurt him. And I can't. So instead I'm going to turn my anger on that unsuspecting girl? That's straight up pathetic. No more. It's time. I hope I'm strong enough.

~~~

He got a little pissy with me. Then thought better of it. I sent him a really good story because I should write porn instead of this shit all day, but also because it was pleasant for me to do.

And my day began with voicemail from Japan. So I'm better equipped to deal with anything Jake.

Signed the guestbook with my name. No love. No call back to the anonymous heart post. Fuck her. Fuck his stupid annoying people. And Fuck him.

~~~

Oh my godddd. The boy from the car...Not sure if it's going past a light alley fingering...which was super hot, by the way. Like I might need that in the mix forever...Anyway...young, hot and I wasn't wrong—absolutely a civilian.

And if the past month turns out to be just another waste of time, I lost five pounds so it's not a complete bust.

I was online this morning looking for a cocktail ring because why wouldn't I want a flower as big as my head for my finger...and Japan appeared...You don't say hi?

Ummm. Like I know he can't see me, but I physically ducked down. I clearly don't know how to disconnect from Messenger, and it freaked me out. But, dude...I'm shopping. You are not on the agenda. Vegas update though. He has to stay on a base for this conference. So that's not going to be a thing for me. I'm not flying out there to hang out alone. I think I might want to date this boy a little. Graham (I think). Date not marry. Like regular people do. Though if I want to ever see him socially, I should probably not indulge in public sex acts every time we run into each other. And maybe also I could remember his name.

Time to pick a fall toenail color.

~~~

I am disgusted by this girl. Just in general. Which I wouldn't even have an opinion about if I wasn't stalking that journal.

Her writing isn't good, and she's not interesting. Is that my annoyance? Maybe.

I read Henry and June this morning. Made me feel way less shitty about my behavior for sure. Also, made me way less concerned with what he's doing. He's training for the next 90 days anyway...but really, big picture and I'm back there, yes...I don't really care.

I'm going out to buy all of the other September issues. Vogue sucked. AGAIN.

Also, new rule...No more uncompensated affection. Wonder if I can get my hair trimmed today. Crazy has set in. Too much caffeine and nicotine. I want him to choose—now. So I can just be done.

I just found ants. That will be remedied immediately. Everything distasteful must be exterminated.

And I'm not sure that it's not Grant...which is weird. And I just cried over an Evanescence video.

What the actual fuck?

~~~

Wine was what. A lot of wine. Gwen and Thomas are having problems. Frankly, I think he's a bit of an asshole. But recognizing my current men are cocksucking liars bias, I did the responsible friend thing and told her to take a step back. Which led to my own near backslide and ultimatum retraction. I didn't. But I was all manner of wanting to say I'm sorry. Please forgive me. None of it matters.

But it does matter. A lot. And if it doesn't matter to him, I can't do it. The end. Enough ink.

~~~

He was the first thought this morning, but fleeting. Now though, I'm way more thinking about my hair. I slept like a stone. And I have to clean and throw away and go to the dry cleaner and the tailor. I'm feeling very Sunday, but it's ok. I have to get those children some clothes and such. I love back to school shopping so much. They won't be nearly as excited as I am, but I'll throw in something to sweeten the deal.

~~~

That crazy dishrag bitch got drunk and posted to the guestbook...which I love too much.

This here crazy bitch got drunk then went out some more, ate dinner, drank water and typed up three handwritten pages of sheer insanity. And I still win. Because my crazy is always in private. It's the kind of insane that actually makes me laugh—when I hover far far above it...Really far.

The boy told me he found a note from Melissa at Jon's that made him sick. My getting this fucked up days have to be over. I'm being totally irresponsible. Tho I never leave my paper where it can be stumbled upon. Grant/am called. I think I have a date this weekend. Weird turn of events. I'm buying a new date ensemble. How is that different from what I wear out? It's new, silly...

Apparently I had to hit extreme crazy to get 70% truth...Three weeks with the dishrag, he claims. 'Let it unwind itself.' So I will because it will. I'm not exactly sitting on my hands.

~~~

Dude. I'm not sure what this mood is. Super aggressive. I think I'm just done crying and giving a shit about these insignificant beings. I sent Jake a movie and then posted as myself. Then I screamed at Jon because he can't manage to do basic shit, let alone one extra thing ever. Baths are such an asskicker, I know. I'm so fed up. I did buy a new copy of The Fountainhead though. Feel like I could use a little hit.

Just had a total meltdown. Very Broadcast News. Purged my system. Purged my phone of boys. Cool with having no one to depend on but myself. Let the games resume.

~~~

Is it a full moon? Am I an 18-year-old boy? Who wakes up like this? Wanna fuck everything. Hard. Like animalistic, throw him down on the floor and fuck his brains out draw blood hard. And it's not love. It's got nothing to do with love. If I was smart, I would hide in the basement and finish Buffy.

Because the 'him' doesn't matter. And that's never a good thing.

Ah, the sweet sound of children screaming at each other...Guess that's one way to kill the boner. Six weeks til Vegas.

~~~

Yeah, so he's got two weeks for it to 'unwind' itself. And then either he ends it or I do. For good. No fucking way that I'm going to deal with this for a year. Somedays I feel like I've stumbled onto a nest of dorks. The family. The dishrag from his office. Him.

C'mon...like you're such a lazy fucker. At least mine was hot. And I didn't let it call itself my girlfriend.

And me...Who am I? A trash chick in his office and I'm like 'Sure, baby. You take all the time you need to let this nothing go away.' Are you kidding? Maybe I care more about bending him to my will than I care about him. 50/50.

Note: I am drinking a wee little bit of wine. If I truly loved him, wouldn't I be forsaking all others? Is it more about the game now? This is a lot of energy, and I'm still kinda bored. Japan is also operating under the notion that I love him. I guess to a point I do, but not in the permanent sense. He's talking in the future tense all of a sudden...I will very much enjoy fucking him without the devotional blinders on. I hope so anyway. I've fucked a lot of people since we were together. A lot of people I've enjoyed. So he'd best bring his A-game.

The more I see of Cutter's family...I mean, no wonder he's so fucking crazy. They're all so very clever. That may be enough to distance myself for real.

Gwen is pregnant because of course she is when she was about to walk out the door and/or bury him in a swamp a week ago...that job might be mine when she leaves.

~~~

No more phantom drama. I need to start living on this plane, without getting fully immersed in the normalness of it all. I want that website up in 8 weeks. That's not very much time. Especially with Vegas and Gwen's Halloween extravaganza in the mix.

Oh, and this girlfriend of Jon's is 23. She's cute. I do enjoy the pierced eyebrow. But 23. No wonder they like her. That won't last.

They never end up choosing the one that everyone likes.

~~~

So I may have to take a little debit in my karma account. I said I was going to leave her alone, but it's just too annoying. I was minding my own business pretty much. Just a throw away 'Hello, hope the weather's great, where you be?' really.

Speaking of dorks, I am having way too much fun mixing my tone and rhythm every time I post. Gotta have a little syntax change-up to keep it interesting.

And then...well...then she fucked up and spoke to me directly on his guestbook. Well, she posted directly after I did. Hi. I'm Dishrag, Jake's girlfriend. I'll update everyone when I have more information. Tsk tsk.

So I might have gone to her journal and mentioned that desperation is a stinky cologne...Because who doesn't appreciate a little Super Troopers reference in a fucked-up, make-believe love triangle?

I'm blocked now on her little Dear Diary page. And much to my petty-ass dismay, it was worth it.

If Dishrag is your soulmate, dude...Have all of it.

Finally got my logo quote. 3 grand? Rapist. Maybe I should have kept all of the artist boys in the phone.

Remember when you were over him?

That's a weird callback. I mean if I think about it, Jake's presence is a product of my unhappiness. After the Tiki Bar fight in California, I was over him. I didn't look for him when we went out. I didn't drunk dial him. I didn't care. I was fine. He left and it was over. And I was fucking content with my life—dare I say happy—until Lucy moved and that fucker's dad bought him my job. Oh, speaking of Lucy, Will is getting remarried. How insane is it that that creep found another woman to marry him?

Anyway...He came back to me after that...Now I'm in this space where I'm not happy and shit is taking too long and I have a stupid day job, and I'm like how can I live without him? Is this another meltdown coming? Two weeks in a row...I'm out of control of my emotions. I feel PMSy, which doesn't seem possible. Let's correct this mood right this very minute. Open the book, bitch. Stop being such a schmuck.

~~~

Finished The Fountainhead. I feel much better. I think this must be what Bible people feel when they read the Bible. So while I'm doing 8000 loads of laundry I will be practicing channeling my inner

Roark...because today, friends, I'm gonna start requiring some integrity flow—to and from me. And at present, I'm not seeing a lot either way. We'll see how we define integrity though won't we?

Lovely trip to the mall. They're ready for school, and mama got shoes. Make lunches. Move car for paver people. Pack backpacks. Give her a bath. In bed and out of my orbit by 8. Highlight: we got the most epic Minnie Mouse costume...70 bucks though for Halloween? I must be out of my silly little mind. Really really cute though. Like I want to wear it. Fucking Disney.

Played grown-up all day. Cab now. And I promised him erotica (because I'm fancy at present), but I don't feel like it. Most productive weekend I've had in a long time. I'm super calm. Scary calm. I don't really recognize it. I feel ok with where we are. Actually, if there's even a we. I'm not so sure. And love...do I love him? Why do I keep asking that?

Lizzie, though. How much do I love her??? She was like bitch, your IP address changes every 30 seconds. She can't block you.

Dark Willow probably could have done without that information.

~~~

He's going going...in a couple of days...Iraq proper. I feel off-balance. Didn't expect that news today. It's not like I didn't know it was going to happen. It just wasn't supposed to happen this fast. And honestly, I'm not sure what I made Kuwait in my head. It's not like he's been holding on a beach in Fiji. I'm a little freaked...God keep him safe. Lotta God of late.

Getting promoted again.

~~~

I'm drunk. Vegas is confirmed. And I'm not really in the mood to be happy about it. I'm feeling very this world is shit. Humans are shit. This war is shit. This mission is shit. I hope he doesn't die in the name of shit. I guess the only choice is to succumb to the shit or triumph.

Did I mention I'm drunk...So drunk I'm slurring my handwriting...

$$\sim\sim\sim$$

Of course I cried my eyes out because emotion overload...or spirit enhanced dramatic indulgence.

Little bit of column A, little bit of column B. It wasn't cute crying either...I'm stupid when I'm drunk. Which is not an encouraging realization considering how much time I spend there.

The dishrag announced Jake's safe arrival in Iraq to the audience. I didn't say or do anything. In fact, I was completely still my immediate, all-consuming hatred. Which must translate to a disturbance in the force even that far away because there was an immediate 'don't even get the idea that I called her' email.

Yeah...that shit'll happen when you're fucking people in your office who have access to information...whatever. I'm just bitter that he put his dick in that.

Repulsed actually.

Oh well. We've all got a couple we'd rather hadn't happened.

Though 'guy in bar next to that gallery' and 'dude in park' aren't showing up on my fucking blog anytime soon.

$$\sim\sim\sim$$

MICHELLE MARIE

Got more direct reports so that lessens my ability to sit and spin in crazy. Missy and Tony. He's cool. Pretty chill and seems pretty capable. She's ok. I don't know. Something's not right about her. And she's his boss so I should probably figure it out.

However, today I also got a war in real-time email. Like Hey...going out to get shot at. Should be back in a few hours. I just sat there and stared at my screen. My hands actually went numb. I wasn't sure that I wasn't going to throw up. Needless to say I'm drinking and trying to decide how I'm going to stop this worry from creeping into a full-time job. I literally just said out loud, 'I wish he was home already and fucking me over.'

That's sad, but at least it wouldn't be this.

~~~

Sunday brings a new war outing...900 pounds of explosives in a truck. He's got a phone now tho, so I don't have to wait for email to exhale. Gotta dry my hair and get ready for company. My like third or fourth or seventh cousin twice removed is coming for dinner. Welcoming all distractions.

This shit is like a roller coaster on acid. What have I done? Why am I doing this? It's going to be so ugly at the inevitable conclusion.

I bought my ticket for Vegas.

~~~

Gwen had a miscarriage. It was oddly difficult to empathize in any real way. Like she's my friend and I love her and I feel bad for her pain, and I was logically very supportive...It happens alot. Something wasn't right. It's not a punishment...Statistically, the next time will be fine.

But I don't know. I sounded sympathetic, but I didn't feel it. It's always strange when I can't tap into a real emotion for something that theoretically I should be able to feel on a real level. Something wasn't right about it...Am I losing my capacity to empathize? Is this shit with Jake making me cold?

You can't like grow into psychopathy right?

~~~

That bitch is not gone. And it's not over. So I have a new game. Every time her dishrag self appears, I will fuck Japan in a more depraved and debauched way...Seems perfectly reasonable.

Had a full on battle with the girl last night about a Hello fucking Kitty shirt that she insisted I must launder immediately for sleeping...at midnight because she's a vampire. She's smart but she doesn't understand laundry cycles, so that shit went into the dryer for six minutes and nighty fucking night. Finally.

Back to School night tonight and tomorrow. Jon will be unable to attend because Germany. Maybe he'll manage to stay in this country for a minute ever.

Also, I am so sick of buying food. As if I don't fucking hate the grocery store enough, yesterday some fat suburbanite screeched at me because she thought somehow I could not see the million-year-old woman with a walker in the road in the daylight.

Sometimes I wish I wasn't actually civilized. I wanted to run her over. The fat one, not the old lady. These people are way too comfortable.

The shitbag was full though I guess because I for sure opened my window and screamed 'You know it's not our fault your husband won't fuck you anymore.' at the absolute top of my lungs. Big karma hit.

Probably gonna have to pay for that one. But fucking honestly??? In fucking leggings and a banana clip? Just don't.

—

Two hours of torture at Back to School night. I thought I was going to cry in science class. Dude, is this my life? No more kids ever...Torture...Wanted to die...and we do it again for the boy tomorrow. Fucking middle school back to school night? I swear to god if they even think for a minute they're going to pull that making me do homework with him every night bullshit...surely that is not a thing in middle school...Oh my god. I will kill everyone.

~~~

Yeah, so I'm not so feeling any sort of pangs about going to Vegas. This is a game to him, and that makes me an idiot...again. I wonder how many 'agains' I've used in the realm of Jake. No matter. I just spent three hours in a text conversation with Jon...is there a chance we could fix this? Fucking you too, dude? Am I just the ultimate in overseas entertainment? The USO should pay me. I felt a little bad. Like I didn't want to say I have no feelings for you because that's not right. I mean it's true, but it's disturbing. Does that make me a fucking psychopath? Ha. Except my drunk for almost a year ass, said sucking phycopath.

He's been gone for five weeks, so I also had to tread lightly or there will likely be another global emergency that only his presence can solve when he should be taking these fucking children. Jake didn't come up. I probably would have lied anyway. Though he's been dating Eyebrow for a while. The double standard is infuriating. I'm so tired of managing their fragile fucking egos. Time for fall toenail changeover!!

~~~

Three weeks til Vegas. Jake update: none. I've been silent and so has he. I do enjoy my throwaway tone, like he's in Jamaica. But he's posting daily, so no imminent danger.

Jon just called and asked me to find his car title...you have got to be joking. Like I'm not actually your admin, sir. You've been gone for a month and a half. Kindly fuck yourself. It's time for all the madness to end. I'm going shopping. Need to make a list. Four days in the desert. My hair is going to be so good!!

Oh my god...Seriously, how is Ross allowed to be open? It's an actual pigsty. Hope I didn't catch anything. Is air syphilis a thing?

~~~

I failed today already. Didn't just look at the blog. Looked and acted. What is actually wrong with me? Maybe Vegas will work like Jake rehab. Cause I am all over the place. I just realized that I haven't slept with another man, not counting a few hours here and there with Jake, for like some stupid amount of years. How is it going to be to sleep with him? So now I won't shit or sleep for four days? Is he a hand holder? I don't even know. I can feel the crazy train gearing up...chill the fuck out. My web address needs to be renewed. And it's fucking raining. I'm livid with myself.

~~~

It was the dishrag's birthday...The only way I'd feel shittier about breaking my silence with him (because I did) is if I had actually sent her the (almost certainly nasty) heads up I wanted to send...on her birthday. It's pointless anyway. I know everything, and I'm still on the fucking hook. Well, I know what I know. I'm sure it's not even close to everything. But Thank You God I am finished with another week of crazy ass work. Anyway, she will find out about him on her own.

No one can tell you anything anyway once you decide you want something

Ahem. Yeah, I know.

Whatever. She's 26. He's a cocksucker. And I damn well know better. Everyone will get what they get.

I'm going to do my work, take my children to the movies, clean this stupid house and then Vegas. Wahoo!

Wahoo??? Who is she?

October

Gwen is pregnant again? Jackie is out of her mind. Why do all of my friends get knocked up? Love is the cheese in the mousetrap. That's a cynical as fuck dating book title. I like it...I should write that...ok also...I have a new obsession taking hold...Adidas? Like not just Yohji. All of it.

I feel like I need to talk to my California peeps. Like I need a little left coast optimism boost...It's working already. Texting with the youngsters...Feeling drunkish on two beers..

That's so fucking weird. Carol called me...from California. The only one I didn't text. I love drunk magic. Oh, and Jake...Jake is saying words that sound sorry. I'd like to think he is feeling a little contrite, but that would be holding on to hope that does not serve me. I don't want to speak to him anymore. Because I can't. I have no ability to not love him. And he cannot be trusted. I want to go out.

Carol thinks Jake will be back. I think he won't...unless he loses a limb.

This year will bode well for you.

Still makes me wanna punch him in the face. What pisses me off is that not only will he eventually be back, but it will be a most inconvenient time...like right after I commit to something else for real.

Maybe Japan—since that seems to be another weird-ass loop of forgetting what I know.

Here's the truth about Jake...Iraq is just a new, more dramatic backdrop. So for all of my fretting and making allowances...Way more than I care to admit to even in here, which is fucking frightening...he doesn't care. Doesn't care. Doesn't respect me. Doesn't want anything real.

Only the where has changed.

Maybe he really is too young.

I didn't really factor that in before because I never factor in fake shit like chronology...but I may stand corrected.

Or he's just Peter Pan...

He's for sure Peter Pan.

~~~

And then my grandmother called me. Which is more weirdness because we call her. That's the rule....And out of the blue, tells me I should never sacrifice my self-respect.

Ummm. I'm not saying my house is bugged, but really? On the day I end it (yes, againnnnn) she decides to phone? It's lovely, but weird.

Took the kids to the movies. Did a little shopping. Hit Taco Bell. And now I'm tired. But my mom tab is paid up. And Jon is staying here while I'm in Vegas, so I now need to gather every scrap of anything referring to anything and bury it all in the yard. Annoying, but it's free. And I guess if I'm being generous...nice of him.

~~~

Woke up with sex on the brain. Surprise. I'm guessing it's nerves, which doesn't make sense. Except that this is about to be not Jake and not just a one-night thing. The eye twitch is back...I'm convinced it's those insane lights in my bathroom. Going to try on the blue cami I got yesterday and if it looks good I'm going back and getting it in silver. The little one in my dream for the second night in a row...Why?

The cami is amazing! Am I taking the brown halter? I need to make a new list...

Andddd two emails from Jake. Thanking me for my generosity...Only one taking care of him over there. I'm the best. Needs to talk to me. Last few emails upset him more than usual...

Not sure what to do about that. So I said if you wanna talk for real and not just manage me, ok.

I cannot understand my inability to remember what conviction is in any real way.

Why would I even listen to one more word?

I was perfectly excited to go on my real life, relatively rational adventure with an actual human who shows up...

Disturbed him more than usual? I don't even remember what shit I said.

~~~

330 AM...nope

815 Dammit

—

625p So beyond busy today. I didn't even have time to consider it. He sent an email to work too. He's very good. Every online bad thing is down...hidden anyway...and the appeal to my caretaker nature was masterful. On a regular day I might not have even noticed. But I'm tired of being the caretaker. I'm also tired of waiting for him. War or not. I don't really even have anything else to say. I'm tired, and I'm done analyzing the virtual nothing that he said.

Now...Vegas. I am getting the silver and that makes my Saturday ensemble kick ass. Hair this weekend.

That lasted...Drunk=right back in it. No. No. No. He knows he's got me...Do not fucking cave.

~~~

Japan called and saved that nosedive. My sinuses are all funky, so daily Emergenc until take off. It occurred to me last night that Japan refuses to learn my number. It's literally the same, one number. I call him all over the goddamned world. Not annoyed. Amused, so that means I'm getting nervous. It's going to be a little awkward at first. Maybe not. Maybe it'll be the most natural thing in the world. How many packing lists am I going to make? I think though that it is complete. Did it only just occur to me that I'm actually also going to have to get ready in the same room with him?

I'm totally excited. And Operation Don't Get Sick is on. No alcohol.

~~~

Forgot to make hair appointment again. And got 'Beautiful' and 'Gorgeous' from Iraq...in lieu of talking I guess. Whatever. That's fine by me. I miss that actually. Even if he's a lying fuck. I'm better, but not where I need to be with that. Going out for a bit tonite.

~~~

So alcohol (not an obscene amount) and a red-headed Columbian...Not sure I knew that was a thing...Hot though. Strangers are such a crap shoot. Bonus—I only spent 16 bucks and clawed the shit out of him. Which I felt baddish about until I did enough recon on his website(?) to see that he has a wife. Which isn't my responsibility.

Not my vows. And not my karma if I don't know...Maybe tho don't take away my option to choose by proactively lying. For sure though don't use your real name and say you're single when you have a website. God, they're so stupid and/or arrogant and/or lucky...til they're not. That took me 30 seconds to find, and only because I had a spelling error. What if I was way more crazy than I am? Japan must be in Vegas now...

It's weird. I always thought Jake would be the first man in the bed.

I feel very ambivalent about last night. I guess it's a good thing that it happened though in a way. I will be much more objective about this excursion. Two notes: Finger in the ass is hot. And 2: I will never ever be able to have sex in this house with those children here. No joke. The walls might actually be made of cardboard. Diz was not amused. Said goodbye to Columbia. And right after I closed the door, he looked right at me and peed on the floor. Fuck you very much too, animal.

Gas, Target and then silver shirt. I'm way excited.

—

So of course-in the tradition of raining and pouring...or feast or famine...or one dick brings many...Jacob called...while I was at the gas station on the way to get the kids. We may have had a little NC-17 chatty chat. He came the hardest...well, maybe ever. And I swear to god, he paused at the close of the conversation—right about where I love you would fit...It was so close and then it was gone. Oh well...Doesn't count after an orgasm anyway.

Gas station phone sex??? Shoulda been gross. Kinda stupid hot. Am I a fucking guy?

~~~

I passed out from exhaustion at 9. Before I could delve into all of the implications of nearly reflexively blurting I love you. And now it's fucking 5 am and I've been up for 30 minutes...This is not going to work.

Now it's 645. Yesterday changes nothing. Exxon Jack and Jill doesn't cancel Vegas. Japan hasn't called yet. He was supposed to call last night. And I'm freaking out a little. Baggage from the last cross country debacle obviously. Maybe I could stay present. At least I'm not driving.

Dude. How hot is Eminem?

~~~

Three days til I get on the plane and no call...I am aware of conferences and how they work, however...I'm just a little out of my mind. What's the worst case scenario? I'll just go alone. Or I'll just go somewhere else...get a car and go back to California. Stop the madness. You are not being even remotely reasonable. Calm the fuck down. I have a lot of work to do today. Huge pile of shit that needs to be handled before I leave.

And I have a big red zit in the most unpoppable position on the side of my nose. Never. Not even in high school, so of course today. Karma.

Also...have yet to locate the condom from the other night. Keep waiting for it to turn up or fall out. So yeah...karma is probably a pretty good answer. Jon said yesterday that he's planning to finish his 20, so he must be thinking about marrying this chick. And since she's 12, she probably wants children so he's decided to choose secure. For the next family. Fuck everyone. Oh, and speaking of secure, Gwen is quitting in August. So that position is mine. I don't have enough time to get the site up by Christmas. Enough. Go to work.

—

Of course he called because that's what people who are true to their word do. They also don't understand why there would be any question that they would...I have to calm down.

I cannot believe I'm going to see him. I can't believe we even still speak.

Now I have to pack all of this paper up and take it to my office (because top shelf of the closet buried under sweaters does not provide ample peace of mind when an ex-husband is staying), straighten up a little, buy sudafed for the flight, clear all the shit out of my computer, and shrink this growth on my nose.

~~~

Oh my...Where to begin? I'm exhausted and a little spacey, but I want to hold the past few days for as long as I can...But first, dinner, souvenirs and bed prep with the children. I even brought Jon a gift.

—

Ok. All is quiet...and I still don't know where to start. With Prince Charming opening the door to the room, kissing me hello and saying 'Nice zit...' Dick. I was furious for about .2 seconds before I laughed like a crazy person because fuck him—I had made it much much smaller...And even though I was mortified, it broke the tension and then it was so good. The hotel could have used a little updating. The hot tub in the room was interesting...At first I was a little like yuck about it, but I got over that remarkably quickly. Way better than fucking on a beach.

So here's the thing...It was really easy. He was kind. And a hand holder turns out. As well as much more of a gambler than I think I understood. I spent a lot of daytime smoking and feeding slots with the old ladies. Not that you can tell what time it is in there. I was also drunk the entire time because I had no idea about free drinks. So drunk for free made my barely there boundaries non-existent. And he fed me from his fork. Not like a whole meal all baby bird like...just when he gave me a bite of whatever he was eating... Which seems like a weird highlight, but it was oddly intimate. I don't know...I loved him once, but it was crazy obsessive infatuation. Now it feels like it could be real? Oh...and the sex was stupid good.

~~~

Oh my god. I am dying...I got the best dark angel costume for Gwen's. Maybe a little too on the nose...Whatever. The wings are no lie almost as tall as I am. Four feet of black feathers??? I want to wear them everywhere. They're ridiculously heavy. And there's no way I can drive in them...Shit, how am I going to pee? I did not factor that in...I should probably watch my liquid intake so I don't flip out and just cut open that unitard at some point...ugh... Should I just switch it up to the black jeans? If I could even find them. They're so tight. No. I can make it like 7 hours without peeing on any given night. We must suffer for beauty. And I'm not buying another pair of stupid black jeans for one fucking party...The ensemble is cute. I'm pleased. Pregnant Halloween should be interesting. She keeps warning me about the brew. Ha.

~~~

I should have eaten more food. Or any...I feel like actual human shit. Whatever death mixture was in that cauldron was no joke. There are photos, so I know I made it through most of the night upright...however...Gwen did ask me this morning as I was crawling up the steps like an animal so I wouldn't puke...wait for it...if I fucked her brother...The little one...He was without question 100% the most interesting person there, so we for sure were hanging out...but the child is 16 or 17. So yeah, no. I'm pretty sure I laughed...It's kind of hard to muster the appropriate level of 'how dare you' when the house is spinning and you have no clue where your bag is. But I do have a few core moral principles that can actually withstand alcohol. Not fucking weird genius kids would be one of them. And even if I was concerned, which I wasn't...I woke up alone under Nana's afghan on the couch in the basement. Fully dressed. Not an ounce of makeup smeared and every piece of my clothing intact. I looked shockingly cute considering...I did briefly wonder if I just peed my pants all night.

She wasn't really asking in any meaningful way. She knew I didn't touch him. Her bitch mother wanted to know.

Dude. I didn't fuck your underage brother. But tell your mom good lookin' out if she thought I was.

Like get up off your ass and find him if you think something's up...Why would you wait til the damage was done? She wants so badly to be the cool, laidback hip mom...Clearly she is not...I don't get people.

I did however get McDonalds...with TWO large Cokes because I'm a genius.

Now my righteously indignant, non-minor-fucking ass is going to sit-sleep in my bed, watch Silence of the Lambs, and try not to die.

—

Should I be mad? Am I mad? I mean I suppose I get it on a concern for your kid parent level, but not as an after the fact data collection point. Whatever.

—

She called and apologized. I was like it's all good. He is actually really hot though. When's his birthday?

Because I knew I was on speaker. And I knew her mom was there. And fuck her.

~~~

Jon's taking the kids trick or treating...He says...I am prepared for either eventuality. He will though...because he loves Halloween, and he gets to score points that I'm sure in his little pea mind makes him Father of the Year.

I took them out on Halloween. Worship my sacrifice.

Wonder how many kids will ring this bell...I'm putting out a bowl.

Is there a Halloween equivalent of Scrooge? The boy was like did you have this bowl out the whole time? Of course not...just while I went to the bathroom... And the girl refused to go to bed until she was certain that she had seen every costume ever made in the history of the world.

Soooooo many kids. Like ants. We need to move.

November

New notebooks make me so happy!!! Really exclamation points? I'm so fucking tired. Not depressed tired, busy tired. So that's better. Work has been crazy. Why did I ever agree to manage humans...There's something not good going on with Missy and Tony. I just haven't figured out exactly what yet. Between them and the lunatics who scream at me and threaten to sue every day...dude...careful what you wish for. Not gonna lie though. I do get great pleasure besting the lawyers...their egos are beyond.

Japan has started talking regularly in the future tense. He's not gotten to we yet though...just I. I'm not sure if he's fishing or just talking. And Jake is behaving like an oddly normal boyfriend? That's fucking ironic. I've kind of gotten used to the war in real time thing. It's still a little surreal and unnerving, but he always checks in when he gets back, so my anxiety doesn't just hang there indefinitely. Though it occurs to me that this is like working two insane full-time jobs. And then I get to come home and continue with a third. The dishrag has been scarce in public. I know she's not great though because I know what he's doing to her (and I might peek in once or twice to the journal just to confirm). Oh well...it'll probably be my turn again soon.

His brother's joining him next month. Just in time for Christmas. So double whammy. Triple I guess if you count Iraq...Today I love him. Jon is taking the kids home for Thanksgiving. I'm going to Jackie's. I'm trying not to be a freak about what she's going to put in the stuffing...I wonder which one will buy the better ring...

~~~

So he sent me a CD. I dig the cover art a lot. I do love a scarlet theatre snap. I'm afraid to listen to it. I'm just staring at it. Like actually just staring at it.

This is never a good thing for me. Music from Jake.

I know it's a trap. This is going to require some wine.

Dude. What the fuck? And now we add Tom McRae to the list of music that will have to be dead to me when this ends.

But for now...is this my love letter? Exactly why I didn't want to listen to it.

He's fucking masterful.

Let's find some ridiculously talented British singer songwriter she's never heard of whose music is fucking haunting and also happens to have some super close to home lyrics that she can attach to and read meaning into for fucking ever. And then send it to her so she can obsess on it in from every angle, including the fact that I physically sent it to her.

I hate him. It's so good. I hate him a lot.

~~~

I made Lily listen to it today at work. I was like what does that mean? You hear this right? This is a trap right? But really good though, objectively. Apart from the messages when you play it fucking backwards...I sounded nuts. I'm sure I looked nuts too when I went flying into her office and demanded that she drop everything.

I really need to hang out with her more. I usually keep my distance because she's Mel's friend. And Mel can be really weirdly pissy about shit like that. But bitch was at a doctor's appointment, so for once I didn't have to low crawl with empty manila folders to avoid an incident.

But c'mon...It is just so calculated.

Oh my god...Literally this cocksucker just said...Oh cool. I didn't even listen to it. I just liked the cover. That's how I've started picking all my music now.

Chill as anything...Which is half believable because I would do that and it is a really cool cover...but also fuck that because he would never put his egomaniac credibility as knower of all things music on the line by endorsing something he hadn't listened to...Nor would he just send me something that may or may not further secure the tether. A book maybe. Music never. He would never leave that to chance. Dude. This level of gymnastics is precisely why I should have thrown it in the trash. Why can't he just admit he fucking loves me? Weakness is infuriating.

Holy shit. Is that what attracted me to him? Is that what I respond to? Japan isn't weak...Is that what attracted me to him? Is that why I can be in this weird dance with both of them? Because I can't choose between strength and weakness? It can't be that simple. Jake was the thunderbolt, though. Japan was not. I don't have time for this...I have to go to sleep.

~~~

How is it Thanksgiving? This is what happens to time when you're old. I have silence in my house for like four days. It is glorious. I just want to sit in it and not move. Gotta get ready to go soon though. I was trying to be all coy and helpful and ask if I could bring anything because Jack is a good cook, but she's not my grandmother. I took stuffing to Thanksgiving potluck last week though, so I'll live if this isn't great. I can't even drink because the road to her house is through the woods and the deer volume is nuts...I hate them. I really should at least choose what I'm wearing. It's going to be pretty low key. Just us and her father-in-law I think.

—

Oh my godddd...I said the most annoyingly Veruca Salt thing I have said maybe ever. And I could feel it as it was coming out. But I couldn't stop it, and I couldn't get it back.

My boyfriend's in Iraq, so I feel just fine about the amount of gas I consume.

Like did you really just say that? I mean...it was an aggressive question meant to make me feel some sort of guilt I guess...but all of my social training totally evaporated. Just fell away, and I went straight, hard brat.

And I didn't soften it. Not even a smile. I just let it sit there and pulled an equally bitchy face. Like fucking yeah, I said that. And nope, not sorry even a little.

And as feared, she put some kind of nut and fruit bullshit in the stuffing. I was unreasonably furious. Maybe I was just a bitch today.

Oh, but I was totally right about those two creeper trucker stalkers in New Mexico or Arizona or wherever. His dad is some kind of state or federal cop...like some sort of task force dude. And he said my instinct was probably pretty spot on. That shit happens all the time. How crazy is that?? I was like I'm sure it was like just me being paranoid. And he was like...it wasn't. And then I was spooked. I was thinking yeah, well another reason you can suck my dick about my gas consumption...I'm not dead in the desert somewhere. But one cunty gas reference in a life is enough, let alone in one meal.

Ugh...Boyfriend? Couldn't even stop it. So ridiculous. Speak of the devil...

God I love that boy. Too much.

December

Jon and the boy are having an issue...It sucks though because it's the same shit I hate about him. So what am I supposed to do? Pretend it's not real, and that he shouldn't be hurt? That seems kind of dishonest. I find myself saying 'no one's perfect' alot. And then being like hey, how about you stop being a cunt to your kid. But that good behavior only lasts for a week. If I'm not constantly on him he reverts to his can't be bothered to consider anyone else thing. It's like housebreaking a fucking dog. Except they eventually learn. Oh, and he's back to Europe on the 26th for a month. I don't even care anymore.

Anyway...tree today. I tried to float the fake tree idea. The boy was like if we don't have a real tree, we should just cancel Christmas. Who are these children? Not that I don't agree in spirit, but could we ever consider anything that might make mommy's life a little easier?

~~~

I'm not sure what's happening, but Jake Cutter just wrote a Haiku...And there's more music coming. I haven't recovered from McRae. This one is different though. I was like another cool cover? And he said nope. It's a surprise. Nothing good can come from this...I feel really strange. Like I'm bored without the fight. Something's off. Maybe I'm anxious about Christmas repeating. Or maybe I just don't trust him.

~~~

Or maybe I felt the embarrassing return of Dishrag to the public forum...Because return she did, in awkwardly fake jokey demanding form about him buying her a Christmas gift...Which was amazing for me to witness because in addition to still keeping tabs on her...because of course I am...I knew he was out doing that actual war thing.

I really don't know what to say when it happens now though. Like sorry your ears are ringing, but other than that the firefight was good? Seems inadequate. And I can't keep saying 'be safe' on a loop. It's annoying. I don't know. I guess I just feel a little lost. Like emotional but not in a real way. In like a button-pushing way. That's for sure boredom. He asked me to find some fabric for him...which I did in about ten seconds...My horoscope said resist the urge to go overboard in my generosity. Too late.

Four hours of dinner and dancing with Santa with the children. I win Christmas.

~~~

That girl just sent my dad an ipenguin. Fucking one-click. Then she realized her mistake...not fast enough to cancel it, but to correct the address and send a second one to the house.

Thank god I logged in because she was about to send a cart full of Barbie shit to Iraq. Which would have been funny if it hadn't been a very expensive cart of Barbie shit. She's a little too smart. I'm going to be afraid of her when she has the mental capacity to cover her tracks. I should dock her list...Kid shopping is done though, so one less thing.

~~~

The Christmas tree has now fallen over twice. Water everywhere. Twice. I almost cried. I'm sure there's a lesson in there somewhere...I'm pretty sure I know how to use a tree stand though, so it's not that...Anyway, Jake has been away for a few days and Japan just called.

Am I faltering in my decision? Did I make one? It was good to talk to him. I felt happy.

Lack of attention makes me fickle.

Gives Attention Deficit Disorder a whole new meaning.

~~~

That fucker is on Dishrag's MySpace. Newly. I will calm down. Better to have caught it now. I can't feel my body and my ears are burning. This fucking liar. And like fucking clockwork, the CD he sent got here. I hate him. Hate. Hate. Did I say hate? Hate. My brain feels like jelly. No tears. Almost. But not. I'm so stupid. So so so stupid. So fucking stupid. He's a liar and a toxin, but I'm stupid. Which is so much worse.

I am not the dumb cunt I play on TV. Sent. First of like five emails, which weren't emails at all but just shitty subject lines with blank bodies.

What is more fucked up though? I am getting a wholly unhealthy adrenaline rush from this. I guess all of my fake moral dilemmas have resolved. I have to stop though. The crazy train, fueled this evening by a second bottle of cab (and pizza, thank god), could derail even harder if I don't get back some kind of control.

TOXIC. TOXIC. TOXIC...

HE IS TOXIC!!! DO NOT FORGET when you're sober.

~~~

Could I have been more drunk? Couldn't even read what was scrawled after that...

113

I just signed on to delete him from my contacts, and he appeared. And then the strangest thing happened...He said Fuck you, I'm sick of this. And something shifted. I wasn't even mad. I was like happy. That he showed a spine. Which was probably not the thing to acknowledge, but it made me laugh.

I was like finally. Let's hear it. Let's have it out. Let's talk some real shit...while you're in Iraq. (Because nothing could be more real than yet another bunch of words from across the world.)

Here's the other thing, though...Like we were pretty honest, and (cautiously) I feel like we may have turned a corner, but it's levels isn't it? Always levels. Like we talk about very specific things that I know he's done. And then I get to pretend to come clean with what I've done that's equally bad, which only amounts to admitting to how I know what he's done. And stalking everyone's online shit isn't all that bad if we're comparing.

So we share our fucked up behavior and apologize. Then we go away and do whatever we want to. I like to think I would have told him the truth about the omitted behaviors if he'd asked.

But he didn't ask. So we aren't real, but I don't want to hate him. Today, I might even like him.

He said I'm like a crazy bitch human version of those white tigers. I will just assume that he meant beautiful and 100% lethal when they decide to be.

~~~

Oh my...Christmas Eve...And the fucking CD. Which somehow I did not destroy in my rage the other night, but did sort of lose til just now. So Fresh Wine for The Horses...Because why wouldn't the lead singer of his favorite band of all time put out a solo album right now?

And why wouldn't the first song be called My Name is Love...And why wouldn't it just get worse from there?

I am 100% being groomed....

And there is an exceedingly high likelihood that I am willingly and actively participating in my own destruction.

—

Just talked to Japan. Ex-wife just sent him quite a whopper of an email...on Christmas Eve. The ex-wife in me wonders what he did.

He listened to my advice this time. And it's strange...Not that he listened, but that I felt some little something. Maternal? Not quite. Friendly? Dunno. It wasn't wanna throw him down on the floor and fuck him energy. I have to clean. He's not afraid of reality though. Jake doesn't love reality. He's kind of allergic to it. I think I'm destined to be single forever. It might be best.

—

And then I talk to Jake for 6 minutes and I love him again. I'm already drunk from one glass of pinot. Amateur. It's time to prep enchiladas and then Cookie Fest begins in earnest.

Fuck. Oh no...I know...I thought I forgot to get bags for the pajamas. I'm like the last person in the world who should have actual Christmas Eve traditions.

~~~

Christmas day. Two pm. Jon's gone thankfully. I'm exhausted. Uneventful sex. Like it didn't even happen. It's raining and miserable, and I just want to lie in bed and watch movies. So I will. Missed Jake.

Sent me a lovely email though. I'm grumpy and annoyed. Christmas I'm tired of saying next year will be different.

Japan called...Again with all of the future talk...I don't know. I feel like I'm cheating. Zero issue fucking, but a conversation...Why do I feel like I've said that like 20 times? Because you have, you psycho. Because it keeps happening...Anyway, he asked me when I'd be over. I am going to have to make some sort of decision. Hawaii holds no appeal. That is a very unpopular opinion in the world of.. well in the world...I'm for sure grumpy. Because now I hate the world and Hawaii. I'm going to sleep and reset this shit mood.

~~~

Second or third chances pay off big time...That was today's post from Jake to his audience. My ego would like to believe that was about us. The rational (ha-is it really?) mind says we're on like round 8, which is way past second or third. So I am now paying attention again. And shopping. Because I want a new camera, and I'm pissed that I have to give up film for digital and still have to fucking buy lenses. The new Canon is like a grand. Fucking racket.

~~~

Two days of silence. My stomach is killing me. I'm so fucking nervous. This was not the right move for me. I can't tell what's causing this. Fear for him or fear of him...Rationally, he said they're not leaving post, but how much do I know about what that means? I've seen how they 'plan'. And how concrete can you be in combat? I guess I can be thankful he's not a Marine. I'd know nothing until it was over. Which actually might be better. I'm going to color my hair. Oh, and there's a blonde. Maybe she's the muse for the second chance. Or third or fifth. Am I losing my hold on reality? Probably.

~~~

Yeah. he's fine. Three days wasted on worry though and doing nothing else? That ain't gonna cut it. On a more positive note, my hair looks phenomenal. Gotta go in and do some actual work today.

~~~

Been almost a week since we spoke...I'm getting sort of tired of this rollercoaster. He's MIA again. We're going to Target...AGAIN. I'm so fucking tired of Target. And AGAIN. I'm especially tired of AGAIN. I'm tired of everything...

January

I wish I did resolutions. It'd give me something to do. Like I don't have enough. If I was only going by this fucking written record (that I just paged through and somehow managed to not vomit) it would seem like I've done little else but lament man drama. Probably because everything else just goes along. The love thing though...that has me flummoxed. I enjoy that word. Flummoxed. Am I bored because everything is quiet? I am skeptical of quiet.

~~~

My admin is pregnant. Not surprisingly not joyous news for her. I was a little taken aback by the weird sentimentality of the independent women in my office who were like are you sure you won't regret this? You could make it work. You're so smart. It wouldn't be like when an idiot decides to have a kid.

Like the girl already said this is not going to be a thing, so shut the fuck up and be supportive.

Is she sure? I almost punched everyone. Just because you had a miscarriage, if that pregnancy was even real...or because your ovaries are cobwebbed the fuck up and there's no dude in sight?? Don't project your shit onto her.

Even Elizabeth, who fucking hates children, was like maybe you should think on it some more...I couldn't believe it. I was like fuck them. Let me know if you need help or a ride. Dude. C'mon. She's like genius level smart working here to pay for school.

She decided. Now she has to pretend to think some more to make you all feel better?

My tone was not pleasant. Only Lily was normal. It was bizarre.

~~~

Japan is still asking about my visit. How does April sound? Sounds like when Jake gets leave...I have been non-committal. Although Cutter has been much more scarce since his playmate got there. Which I expected, frankly. That brother dynamic is very Peter Pan Permission Slip in any context. Add in the whole 'I ain't dead yet, so I must be invincible' thing and it really just becomes a matter of time.

It isn't going to make it hurt less, but maybe if I'm prepared for it...

Does anyone believe that?

~~~

Holy shit. Dickinson is playing. Gig and I are going. Don't think for a minute I didn't post that news for his audience because I knew he would respond reflexively. And he did. Immediately. And then I posted right under him and signed my name with all the cute anonymous call backs I've used for months. Check and mate, Dishrag. He's not good with truth...and not only do I exist...I actually am the one who's not that nice. And boom goes the dynamite...

He knew I would do it for him eventually. I need to add an Unwinding Fee to my Services Rendered invoice.

~~~

Could it be PMS again? Sunday can never completely be overlooked as the culprit...So as I was running errands thinking about how much I hate having responsibilities, I was noticing the men pushing strollers...none of them looked happy. Like at all. Like they all were forced to participate. Why do men want children? Do men want children? Does anyone really want children? Like as an end-all be-all? Are there people whose lives are truly made whole by having them? Trina for sure isn't like that. Jackie is all aboard that 'now I know why I'm on the planet' train...That's never been me. I bought some shark shit to fade stretch marks. Let's see how that goes. Jake countdown is on...I need to get to divorced. Oh right, and start this company. Gigi is a total wreck right now. And it's pissing me off. Two appointments. That's all I needed her to make. Literally how can people who have no one to manage but themselves not get simple shit done? If all I did from my daily shit list was get three people ready for the day factoring in food prep, money and tantrums...I would still get more done. I'm through with compassion.

~~~

Had a bath and massaged in the gunk. It smells like fish. It's fucking appalling, but there's no one here to smell me so I may as well get over it if it works. If I could not dry heave, it might be ok. Fucking shark oil. Did I think it wouldn't smell? I wonder if it's bad. How would I know?

The boy just came up to pretend hang out so he could ask for pay per view. He's cute. At least he asks. If he was really smart he would ask that girl to steal it for him on the neighbor's account or whatever alternate internet universe she's probably using. I'm out of wine. I wonder if I can not drink for a night. 　　　　．

Nope. How then would we create such fucked up porn? So not a chance...That one outdid itself. Tho why I write anything at all for him is a mystery. Maybe it's really just for me to get off.

I kinda feel bad for Dishrag. What's wrong with me? Maybe I just know too well how it feels to be in the web. I tried to warn her.

And when it's my turn? Really—I wouldn't be doing this if I didn't believe this was it. Like it it. Bound forever it...

If he doesn't flake. It's still entirely possible. But why would he?

Why would you count on him not to? Because you love him wif your whole widdle heart?

And that...That's exactly how come we should try not to drink for a night.

February

Fuck this suburban shit. This ends today...I caught myself wanting to trade lives just for like an hour with this group of college kids in line in front of us at the diner. Not that they were anything overwhelmingly special. They were just kids. But something about them made me instantly aware of how stupid thrown together the three of us looked.

And of course you can't be like "We're leaving now. Your slovenly appearances create a stench of complacency that mommy cannot tolerate."

It wasn't that bad. It was worse. It was just normal. It was as if I had conceded to this boring as fuck fate. And that's not gonna work for me. I may live here, but I don't have to conform. And they sure as fuck won't either. We are going shopping.

Japan called, and the girl calculated that she would get her way if she threw a tantrum right that second. I wasn't nice, nor soothing, nor calmly firm, so not an ounce parental. She's not getting that computer. It makes her completely unhuman.

He said I hope you're not taking care of me someday. And I said well presumably you're not gonna whine at me for three days when I take something away from you that's rotting your fucking brain. I was in a frenzy, so I do not count that as any sort of 'we have a future' exchange.

I just ate a ridiculous amount of food and now I'm listening to Dickinson. I'm going to have to choose. Not really a choice though is it?

I know I can't be completely objective and say that Jake doesn't factor in here, but I'm not sure I want Japan anymore. I mean...even if Jake does flake...we've met me...it's not like I won't meet the fourth love of my life. I fucking love everyone.

~~~

Dishrag's friends are pisssssed at him—one of them called him ass-face in her diary. That's funny. They'll kill him. Reason number 754 why we don't shit where we eat...especially when we gotta go back...Whatever. Fuck him. I have so much to do. Regular work...paperwork to file. Descriptions to write. PayPal accounts to open. Bills to pay. Divorce decrees to download. And I'm tired of my own voice. I'm going back to yoga.

Japan asked when we were going back to Vegas. I find myself annoyed at that memory.

She deleted the ass-face comment. Pussy.

I know he's a selfish cunt. But aren't we all just a little...I mean I for sure want what I want. And I don't fucking care what anyone thinks about it. Nor am I super interested in what anyone else wants.

Maybe I'll write The War in Iraq: A Love? Story. It grows on me a little more with every glass. Maybe he can write it with me...I can't ask him though because then I've manipulated the outcome.

Who are you kidding? You want to tether him just like he's tethered you...silly, silly, drunk bitch. That's cute, but you're fucking unhinged when it comes to this one.

Did you just call him your muse?

Cork the fucking bottle. Jesus Christ.

—

Just texted Mimi. She had the abortion today. That makes me sad for her. Just that she had to go through it. I just asked her if she's eaten. Is that like such a my grandmother thing to say? That's a bizarre shift...Love to abortion...really though I love her, so I guess it's kinda not that weird. She's probably more deserving of my energy in truth. I'm way too close to that situation.

Fresh Wine and actual wine is not my best move.

~~~

Said goodbye to him today. For real. No ultimatum. No nothing. Because apparently I do have a limit.

He'd best hope I can keep my shit in check long enough to not dance in the public square of that blog. Motherfucker on that dating site. Actively. He changed his screenname to a gay brit popstar. Sounds about right. But I found him. Both of us gone in two weeks. I ended Dishrag, and he ended me. Well, I ended me, but either way, that's pretty fucking impressive.

Spineless, weak, pathetic piece of shit...that sounds familiar...oh right. Last year. This year—no puddle. I'm fucking livid. Flew right the fuck past rage.

Like the next time I see you I hope it's in a box in Arlington level fury.

Of course I would never.

Some things you can't undo.

—

And then I calmed down. I copied his most heartfelt email and asked 'Bullshit All?'

Then came the fucking tears. So many tears that Japan asked me if I was sick...Nope. Just bawling over a boy that you will never know anything about. No more tears. No more consideration. No more fucking wallowing. Not another word ever...Walking disaster area, indeed.

My muse?

My ass.

Relationships end all the time—too fucking bad. I took a chance. I was wrong.

~~~

Grieving period is over. I do not look pretty when I'm puffy. One big meltdown is enough. My head hurts, but I drank a lot last night. And I actually got a lot of work done today, so let's shake off this Jake funk once and for all and move on.

One thing is for certain, there will be no more 'hi' and 'big picture' and 'life's too short' because frankly *my* life is too short.

Mimi is leaving. Not shocked. I'm glad for her actually. She's too smart to get trapped in this vortex of crazy.

~~~

Know what's so fucking annoying? I had this lovely fantasy of asking his favorite musician in the world, who will be ten feet away from me to do something. I'm not sure what...Picture. Phone call. Email. It wouldn't be hard. Now, however, I will not because he does not deserve any such consideration. But I'm annoyed because I wanted to do it as like a really nice thing and he's ruined it, and I hate when anyone's behavior gets in the way of my natural inclination to do something thoughtful.

Whatever...He'll be fat two months after he gets back anyway, so...Public humiliation, bitch. You have one actual rule...No faltering. No more. It will always be just one more email. One more hi. One more excused slight. One more time. One more 'Maybe this time'.

Jon isn't taking the kids this weekend. He's got a birthday party. I hate his fucking guts. Japan is saying sweetcheeks to me...I think it's in jest. It better be...

No more JakeWatch either after today. It's unhealthy. Though I gave myself this one last pass because how else would I know that all of his contraband liquor got confiscated. Ha. Karma is global lover. Suck it.

~~~

I need JA. I can't stop writing hate email. I'm not sending it because it's horrifying and thats not who I am...

Ate a bologna sandwich and got past the urge.

March

Interview today. New boy admin. I'm hiring him if he has even half a brain. Because I have to go in on a weekend to file? No fucking way.

~~~

He replied to Bullshit All?

You know it probably was. Who knows what I want from one minute to the next.

And I think I'm a little stunned because I think it's probably the first time he's ever told me the truth.

I hired that boy admin. Curt. He's kinda cute in that dorky, gamer kind of way. I'm drinking vodka. Tim will be back for the summer soon. Office full of boys. I'm all about this shit now. Temps don't count in the whole inappropriate thing do they? Whatever. I'm not going to fuck him. I might want a flower shop.

~~~

Gwen and I went out for a little. Which isn't as fun because pregnancy. I'm starting to feel a little despondent. Because I know it's really over. And I hate him, but it's really like hating a ghost because he just told me that he is bullshit. And if I was wrong about him, am I wrong about Japan?

Whatever. That is over. It's over. No more. Wrap your head around that and move on. No more checking. No more visits to his people's spaces. Could I just convince myself that he's dead?

~~~

Found another pretty cool house. But it's a shit elementary school. Can't do that. So I guess I'll stay here and piss away my money until I can get the good house and the good school. Japan is going to be gone for like all of next year.

I just spent six hours filing. Fucking filing. That's not great for the brain not spinning on horrible mean things to do to the ghost of Jake. I won't.

Instead you're going to pay your bills, start your company, actually divorce your husband, and maybe go to Vegas again. Sounds better.

Japan lost his phone for three days. Who does that? Is it weird that I didn't notice?

~~~

I have started to judge every syllable that Japan utters now. I mean it's not like he's an idiot. He's a pretty smart dude. Not crazy smart, but what have we learned about crazy smart? It's still fucking crazy. And whatever fucked up thing my brain is doing...like surely I can find another physical specimen like Jake...which would be the equivalent of fucking him and that would be pathetic and sickening. Doesn't matter. We all know his fat tendencies. Sure, he's beautiful now but that ain't gonna last. And once he's fat, I won't care.

Here's the thing...do I go to the show? I have the meetings too. That I have to set up because of course I do. Though I'm not sure I want to do business with people who can't seem to get their shit together for shirts. Is that hard? It's your actual business...Not sure I understand the obstacle there.

I'm going. I paid for the tickets. I have people to see. I should just give Gig the tickets and go see my grandmother. My stomach hurts. Maybe it'll be cathartic.

~~~

So, yeah...I did not see my grandmother. Should have. The meeting went surprisingly well. Got what I needed and have a vendor. Other dude was a no go. Had lunch with Trina. Those are the sober anchors in what I wouldn't quite call a mistake because I'm alive. Ten years ago I would have just called it a night, but now...'not my finest hour' doesn't seem adequate. The half a tab of acid maybe wasn't my smartest move. But that was somewhere in the middle of my fucking weeping through Rob Dickinson's entire show...which if my calculations are even close—was 9 hours into the bender, so it didn't really matter at that point.

And yes I said weeping. And no friends, not silent streaming tears. I fucking wish. Actual hard crying. From the first fucking lick to the end. In a bar. And not a dark bar. Like not even a real bar. A fucking restaurant that turns into a bar that turns into a concert venue for a dude with a guitar. Not a band. A single dude.

Gigi kept apologizing. To everyone.

The chick who has always been the mess and never fucking says she's sorry...She felt the need to apologize. For me. To strangers.

Flashes keep coming back. Like some drugged out montage because real talk, that's what it is.

Nothing after the show is clear. I'm pretty sure we almost started a fight in a bar. I remember the boyfriend saying he couldn't hang out with us anymore because we were trouble and going to get him killed. The only things I really know is a) G and I went to that show and b) we didn't fuck each other.

Unimportant but weird side note: I met a dude who owns a jag dealership somewhere. Bizarre. Called me on my drive home, so I obviously gave him the number. I'm not sure what kind of accent that was, but it hurt my head to find basic words. I just hung up like in the middle of my own sentence.

There was a party. Or two. And a fire escape. Hands and mouths and bodies...Different hands. Different mouths. Different bodies. Fragments. I'm not sure any of it even happened...Maybe I hope none of it happened.

Made it to our hotel. Woke up in our room. Not missing anything and not bleeding from our assholes...That's usually a joke. Today it wasn't.

—

I'm just sitting on the couch. I haven't moved for an hour.

I'm trying to remember. Trying to get the movie to play. Trying not to walk over to the computer to tell Jake about the show—minus the sobbing. Trying to decide if this giant glass of wine will be enough to magic me back to the part of my fucked up brain that's holding the real story. Or if it's just gone. And I should let it be gone because it's for the best...Trying not to cry some more. If that's even physically possible.

What I'm really trying not to do...

I am trying not to scream.

—

Then I did. Metaphorically I suppose. But with nary a blink of my red, puffy as fuck eyes—I broke my Cutter ban and my crazy in private rule. Because...oh, yes there is.

There's another onnnnnnnneeeee. Not even that newly surfaced blonde one. A new new one. And he just publicly declared himself to be in an actual relationship with it...To all of his people...so I responded in kind.

The show was amazing!!!

Oh...and I fucked your god. xoxo

—Fade to motherfuckin black, bitch—

Does anything rhyme with donkey punch? Nothing real. Completely unrelated to that...Why is everyone sending poetry of late? Japan's ex sent him some kind of love poem. I didn't ask if she wrote it because I don't really care and couldn't make asking not sound shitty, and I'm working on managing my snark factor.

Jon's leaving for another month. I hate him. He asked me to take him to the airport, and of course he beat me to the house and this was lying open. He knows that rule though...you read it, you own it. Not for public consumption. It's a fucking moment in time. Though I'd prefer no one else own the last few months. And if I was smart, that last entry should probably be set on fire.

Trina, this lunatic, asked when I would stop being self-destructive about love...Ha...She was probably calling me from the boyfriend's bed. That's gonna be ugly when it blows up.

Oh my god...What in the world is happening? Japan bought me a gift. It's probably a golf glove. If I wasn't so angry at seemingly everyone and everything, I might be happy that he bought me anything.

Went to lunch with Jackie and the baby. This baby thing is going to get old real soon. And by soon, I mean it is. Her husband is sleeping in the basement because she has that infant in the bed. He'll have a girlfriend in six months...I smoked too much today. And I'm drunk again. Way too much. Too much. So much. Again. Story of my life.

Dude. Why is Jake trying to talk to me? Just leave me alone. I couldn't have made it any easier. I am clearly insane. And I've done enough for you. Absolution isn't on the menu. My resolve hasn't weakened, but I can't hate him today. That's annoying. I gave Jon dentist and doctor appointments because that's a task that he can manage and it takes it off my plate. Japan texted and I didn't respond. I didn't want to...Am

I self-destructive? Whatever. I'm grumpy and I have to order business cards and look into bar codes.

Oh, and all of a sudden, that boy child is taller than I am...Did I fall asleep for a year? Ha. Sorta.

April

I wrote 10 new cards last night. Had Dickinson on a loop. I gotta beat it, so its not ruined forever. Not there yet. Maybe it's a little too soon. Anyway, ten playfully nasty greeting cards is much better than directly unleashing more rage. I'm way too excited about the new dick one...So until the desire to take a bat to him passes, I guess we'll just create.

Though what will I use for inspiration in the absence of him fucking me over?

The 20 other CDs and every email and text and voicemail you have?

Warrior Yoga sounds like it might be just the thing. I need to be mainlining yoga at this point.

Why do people do the 'a friend' thing? Just say 'my friend, John'. It's infuriating. Like whoever you're hanging out with isn't so cool and mysterious that you cannot identify them, Japan. I swear to god. Am I supposed to ask if it's a chick? I don't fucking care, dude. But my threshold for fucking games is over. I don't think this is going to work. Going to watch TV and stop thinking.

~~~

I woke up angry this morning. That's new and different. He called to see if I was having a better day today. What the fuck ever. I'm not talking to him. Am I feeling better? How about you just don't speak and I'll be fine. Hey, hostile. Feeling very hostile. Like make someone pay hostile. Going to Chili's with Mel and Lily tonite. Ha. That should make it all better. Or I'm going to stab the first person who even sort of glances in my general vicinity because...Chili's.

~~~

More unhappy dads...it's an epidemic. Though it was Chili's, so maybe it's that. We had fun, though. I think my flower shop will sell 'you're a fucker' bouquets. All the dead flowers that didn't get sold...Japan is being nice so I should probably stop being mean. Also, who knew clothing labels were such an ass kicker? Why is this a thing? Fucking find them. I might have to ditch bender meeting guy. Hahahahaha. I can't remember his name. it's something short like matt or john or mike...Tonite I hope that Jake is in a very dark, very deep pit of despair. So that's a cool flash of not kindness.

~~~

He may live...Matt. That's bender meeting boy's name. Yay me. He's sending my logo today. Is Japan dumber than I thought? It's easier to see now. I don't know...I don't care a lot though, so it's really just a note. Fell asleep and missed the Sopranos. My face is itchy. Is it early enough for allergies? Or maybe I've finally developed an allergy to the pinot.

Oh and the girl's little friend...her dad called me and talked to me for three hours...Another less than pleased father. Am I attracting them or just noticing more? Lord knows I'm not all energetically open from yoga since I haven't been on a mat for ughhhh I don't even want to think about it...Whatever. They're getting divorced, so I thought he just needed someone to talk to, but it kind of started to turn...said I was very attractive and that Jon would have a very hard time replacing me...like that's even possible. I didn't bite though. And he's actually kinda hot and getting divorced, so I was annoyed that I was annoyed...I don't know...I think I resent anything even resembling usery now. You wanna fuck me, ask me out. Don't boohoo at me for three fucking hours. What kind of sad-ass foreplay is that?

Japan's cholesterol is 220. I have no idea what that means, but they put him on a diet for kidney patients so it ain't good. He's a little too young to be getting old man diseases. I don't need to be taking care of that. I'd pay someone to though maybe.

Listened to Fresh Wine. Didn't really cry. It was comforting kind of. Like rubbing a bruise. It hurt, but not as close as it did. It's getting duller, the pain.

Gig and that dirty boy broke up. She's in a hole. So I guess all of the assistance we all were pretending she was going to provide is back on me. I anticipated as much. I just wish this wasn't the reason. I'm sad that she's sad, but he's a piece of shit so...

~~~

Jon is leaving now for the entire summer. Fuck my life. And then Japan says he's considering being an EMT in some ugly brown fucking corner of California? What is happening? I don't have time for this pretending to care about options that are just fucking stupid. I hung up on him. He can go do that, but not with me. Actually, he can do whatever he wants because he's not my boyfriend.

Hey, there's a newsflash girl. He's not your boyfriend.

~~~

Or I'm going to Hawaii in two weeks. And Jon's mother is coming to stay. Five hundred bucks, and away I go. No time to stress. No time to diet. No time for anything. Just going.

~~~

How do I have a middle ear infection? Do adults who don't swim even get those? Five days is more than enough to clear it up. Drops and antibiotics, which I hate. But I'd rather not have my eardrum explode.

I'll just eat sudafed and claritin and very pointedly ignore whatever warning this might be.

~~~

The girl just threw up all over CVS. Just random threw up...She's fine now. And I feel really bad. She was freaking out, and I was trying to comfort her but I was laughing like an asshole with my hands full of vomit. I couldn't stop because it was so insane. The two of us just standing there. Nowhere to go. Fucking surreal. Sweet, now I also get to avert a yeast infection...

His tone is different tonight. Not asshole. Not giddy...I can't quite figure it out. He's picking up his new bike tomorrow though so he's happy. Weird. Is happy the tone I've never heard? What the fuck are we going to talk about when there's no Vegas?

Oh...and he said I'd better be able to cook because I'm going to be doing a lot of cooking??? Is this some kind of domestic audition? Cause bitch, I've been cooking my whole fucking life. That's not even the point a little...

Is this a mistake? Probably. Unfaithful is on...Ha. There are no mistakes. Only what you do or don't do. I feel like I should have read more Sartre because it sounds a little cribbed from a philosopher. Or dude is just French. I'll take it as a sign.

Of course you will. Not your first ear infection in 30 years or your child puking in the pharmacy without any identifiable cause, though? We'll just ignore those.

~~~

Five days... My ear feels better. EmergenC, water, and yogurt. Babies can fly 48 hours after they have antibiotics, so I'm not super pressed on it. Though I am going to max out my immune system. If I ate like this all the time I wouldn't be fucking sick. What is this Jake gnat? Distanced, but buzzing for sure. How much more fucking garlic can I consume? Bought new underwear. And all of a sudden I am aware that he's auditioning as well. Unfortunately for him, it's like the opposite of whatever June Cleaver shit he's got in his head for me. I'm not sure who he thinks I am, but I feel like it's not even close to reality. Oh, and I'm missing the Ball by a day. How am I missing another ball? Always just missing the opportunity to get dressed up and dance. A hundred years with military men and the only associated thing I would actually get any pleasure from, I never get to do. My timing is bizarre.

~~~

Well...that was interesting. Hardly what I would call a vacation. Highlight: I won a poker tournament...because men are simple, moreso when they think a girl doesn't know the rules. So I made money on this trip. I did cook twice, and I'm not sure who he's been with before, but they clearly had zero talent. I didn't even try. It was like Home Ec: The Middle School Years.

Let me not bury the lead. I'm not fond of him in reality, and this has pretty much run its course. Which is funny because I used to tell Jake that if he would just stop being a lunatic, we could have already broken up for a real reason in the amount of time we've wasted.

First two days were ok. Went out to dinner. Did the poker thing. Had sex. I even went golfing. Well, I drank and read Skinny Legs in the cart. More sex. Then came the unraveling.

The first fight was about the insinuation that I said he didn't have to use a condom because I was potentially trying to get knocked up to trap him. I may have overreacted.

But it actually wasn't even an insinuation. He straight up said, why do you not want me to use a condom? Are you trying to get pregnant? And I was like ummm...are you out of your fucking mind? It's because anal doesn't result in a kid, idiot...Not only do I not want any more children, I would never ever everrrrr have your stupid fucking general ed baby. And if by some fucking dark magic that were to happen, I would only be pregnant for the ten minutes it would take me to drive to the clinic.

I stopped short of calling him microdick...but only just. Almost bit my little tongue off.

So yeah, the rest of the night was a little tense...He did apologize in the morning. A lot of chicks blah blah blah. It didn't help. I wasn't hearing it. I should have moved my flight right then. Why would I listen to my intuition? Where's the fun in that? Then I would have missed the motorcycle ride in the bitch seat...at top speed. Because he thought I was joking when I said it scares me to be on the back of a bike? Nah...he did it as payback. I don't know how I fell for it again. Jon did it too. It's like the only place they have any ability to actually feel power over me.

So we didn't speak the rest of that day either. Well, not after I flipped my shit about the bike...and he told me to calm down because his neighbors could hear me and I sounded crazy. What is about that word that makes you double down on both volume and intensity? Cause I did. I was like I don't give a flying fuck about what anyone who can only afford to live here thinks of me. Fuck them. Fuck you. You didn't want a fight you should've thought about that before you scared the living shit out of me...You don't want your neighbors to hear you sneeze, you shoulda bought more land. It was bad. He went to work the last day...or somewhere...and then came the shit icing on the cake of fuck that was this week.

Wait for it... A fucking Christian singles account. Christian...This heathen...And the fucked up part was that I wasn't even snooping. He told me to use the laptop. Well the really fucked up part was that I knew immediately why that site. It's got everything to do with him wanting someone who sees him as the king to be served and nothing to do with God. His profile was so full of shit that I felt sorry for him.

That's not exactly true. I felt like this cocksucker, who I may or may not murder, of course that's what he wants. Don't we fucking all?

I was calm though when he got back. Didn't even mention it. Because why would I fight about something that's just so gross? And then we installed new lights in his fucking ceiling. Like with power tools and dust.

And the whole time I was thinking you have got to be kidding me. Whose life is this? Not mine...But thank you for this glimpse into fucking bullshit domestic snoozeville. Like sure, anal is easier when it's like the equivalent of a finger, but participating in actual home improvements??? You're way better off with whichever one of those website chicks you con into believing you're a man of God...fucking please.

All I felt when I was finally taking off...This is a long-ass flight for some scenery.

~~~

My mother-in-law said that Diz saved her life...so that's good, since he ate all of the Easter candy she brought for the kids out of her suitcase. I'm not sure if it happened or she dreamed it, but I was like I guess if it's a choice between knowing not to run into a bus or eat cigarettes and sniffing out and alerting you to a potential diabetic coma event...We're calling him Diz the Wonder Dog now. I've never seen him open the refrigerator, and god knows that would've come in handy more than once...but honestly, who the fuck knows what strange shit is possible. I did toss a 'bless this house and keep them safe' before I left.

~~~

What just happened? Japan text

With what? My answer. Cause I am not about to own anything...I thought we were finished. I am finished. But I guess this is closure? I don't know. I don't care..but if he wants to talk. I guess I can talk. Or write while he talks.

Nah. Text.

Why was that so bad?

Because you clearly don't trust me or worse, you think I am the type of person who would get pregnant on purpose. Either way it's not good. Then you called me crazy and told me to keep my voice down when I had every right to be pissed.

Can we talk?

I can't talk. I have people here. Maybe later.

OK

I don't have people here obviously. But fuck him. And also, I haven't processed how I feel about it. Or if I even feel anything about it. Is this jet lag?

~~~

I had some vodka before the actual call.

I don't want to fight with you. I just said it. I didn't really mean it. We had a lot of port. I don't think you'd really do that. My ex is putting me through some shit...two alphas are going to butt heads...blahblahblah.

(I mean she is. I've seen it...but I'm not her.)

Said I'm not some high school hillbilly from your hometown. If you can't make that leap, we don't have anything else to talk about. Maybe you need a different type of woman...maybe a more like white picket, god-fearing woman...

He didn't bite, so maybe he didn't mean for me to see it. Is that worse? Whatever...oh, and he did buy me a bracelet. I forgot about that. Me, the lover of gifts, forgot...It's jade...and not awful.

Anyway, he apologized and I didn't. Because I'm not sorry. And it's not worth my energy to continue. Maybe if he gets entertaining really quick, and that's unlikely because he's deploying in an hour...I'm bored with this...He said he's coming in June. At least here I know where to bury a body.

And for the record, silly little man...

There is only one Alpha.

May

Gwen is leaving leaving for good once she has the child...We have a new boss from the mothership...I like him though. He's like grounded smart, but really actually smart and not just some shady corporate stooge like the last one. He's got that street kid made good vibe. I would've guessed Chicago, not Boston. Although I don't really think I know anyone from Boston so maybe...I have to go to Philly for a conference. They're sending me into the belly of the beast to represent the most hated organization on the planet. I'm not super excited by the thought of one of these people punching me in the face...or even really knowing what my face looks like...

~~~

My grandmother died. Apparently she was in the hospital while I was in Hawaii and told them not to tell me. Not to ruin my vacation. Which was so sweet, but makes me so sad and so hateful that I was spending that time with that bullshit when I could have been with her. I'm not taking the kids to the funeral...I find the whole viewing thing kind of barbaric and creepy now, especially for children. It's not the same as it was when we were little...We went to a funeral every other week. It was just a thing we did...They've never been to one. I don't think this will be the first. Not with my having to be there for all 6?? of the viewing sessions...and also, love them as I do, not with this family without my grandmother there to referee. Jon concurs, like it fucking matters.

Do I even have four days of appropriate costuming for this?? I have like six hours to get it together before I have to leave for the airport. Fuck me.

~~~

Good call on the no kids at a wake decision. If for no other reason than the mixture of grief and family secrets and Jameson. Thought for a minute we had been fed a whole lotta Jager...or acid...Silly rabbit that I am, I changed my ticket to the next day when it was still good times. Shoulda felt it coming. It went from fun reunion cousin kumbaya to screaming 'I saw the texts. I know about her.' Almost to the second, as I was hanging up with the airline.

If we all had dicks, we would have just been standing around with them in our hands. Is there a co-ed word for that?

Duhhhh? We were all just one big collective Duhhhh. And it just slid into 50 years of shit from there. Who's been fucking who and for how long. Who stole what cash from what account. Who would finally be exposed as a criminal when the will was read. Who should shut the fuck up because their ex wife wasn't exactly faithful except maybe on their wedding night. Who wasn't ever loved or even wanted for that matter. Who never got the first piece of fucking cake...even on her fucking birthday.

I'm sure my grandmother was pleased. She was always such a fan of family business being shared with the world. And outside where shit doesn't get muffled even a little. Made it so much better. She'll be haunting them hard for embarrassing her like that.

Gotta say though...As adult grandchildren, we were all in agreement...It was perversely spectacular to watch.

Drama cuts quite nicely through sadness. I was up and out at the asscrack...Called a cab. Smooches...You all can recover from whatever that was or is without me...Fucking psychos. Love you. Bye. Almost puked in the taxi. Special kinda hell that.

Nothing good comes from brown liquor. Ever.

Oh...ummm...speaking of...I slept with Lafferty the night before. Kinda by accident, but not really. I pushed. I blame Jameson. Well maybe more like the spectre of Jameson because I was drinking vodka. That was really just one of those inevitable things...it should have been consummated a long time ago. It was good, though. A little weird. Reminded me of the night I finally saw Alvin Ailey...Like objectively it was Alvin Ailey, but I had been waiting so long that the reality could never hold up to the feeling I thought I would have.

Probably would've been hotter if we had done it back in the day when we were too young to let grown-up, self-conscious shit inhibit us...ha...or rather when he had no grown-up self-conscious shit more like it. Who knows though. He's always been kind of reserved. Took 15 years to break through that wall. I was 50/50 on gay. If I'm honest, I still don't know for sure.

I'm waiting to see what perspective changes now...I usually get some sort of life is too short bug in my ass after a major death. Last one ended my marriage. And this is my grandmother, so it's weird that I'm...ugh...no. Nope. No. No. Fucking no you will not. Jake does not get to come back in. Focus elsewhere. Job. Kids. House. Fucking business??? New hair. Maybe a bob? Anything else. Not him. Don't you fucking dare.

~~~

I didn't. I may have taken a teensy peek though. Just to make sure he was still alive. He is...But not saying anything—that was a fucking battle.

Gwen's last day is today. I told her I would shoot her Demi Moore Vanity Fair pregnant cover moment. I hate shooting humans, but it'll be fun. And presumably, god willing, she won't be naked.

Baby means no more going out ever, and now we won't have work, so for all practical purposes that's a wrap on that chapter.

~~~

Well...I am breathtakingly sad. Shattered actually. Because for the first time in a long time, I have been betrayed. Not romantic Jake has four girlfriends and Japan is looking for a butter churning farmhand fucked over...Real affect my actual life betrayal...by one of my best friends.

Is there anything that can drag you back to high school quicker? Back to the person you know you aren't anymore...The one who didn't give a flying fuck about your tender feelings and was so fucking mean, like soul level mean. Like know your deepest shame and poke you in it repeatedly, from all angles every day until you curl up in the fetal position and cry...That's the level of dark I am feeling right now.

Gwen...This bitch...This bitch whose job Mel and I have been doing for the past six months. And for real, not just like when people think they're doing more than the boss. Bitch has been shopping and decorating her nursery. This dumb cunt thought she would negotiate a nice consulting gig for her oh so brilliant and talented and irreplaceable ass by saying that Melissa and I are not capable without her...The fucking nerve. I can't even write. My hands are shaking. Because I'm all for her getting an unnecessary paycheck...but at least get it by being creative in your fiction...Not by fucking painting us as incompetent. And she's lived in her little my mommy told me I'm the smartest girl in the room bubble a little too long because Boston? Boston saw right through that shit and came to us and said Gwen says you're not up to the task and that she has to stay on as a consultant for the health and stability of the company.

And then he met the real me and got exactly what he needed. The truth about who has been running this shit. And her little plan to bend us over the table and fuck us in the ass and collect a hundred grand was foiled to fuck.

~~~

Oh my god...She doesn't know that we know. Because I just had a perfectly normal conversation with her. The fucking balls on this chick. The maternity photos I shot are fucking stunning, by the way.

I'm kinda pissed now that I didn't fuck her brother.

Yeah...we're gonna drink. We're gonna drink, so that we pass out and don't text, email or scream even one of the vile things we could at her about every ugly thing we know will level her to the ground...because that is not who we are anymore. And we take the high road and she gets nothing...Checkmate. You absolute fucking soulless devil hook-nose poodle-headed bitch.

~~~

Wow. Someone was a little angry. Ha. I am now the boss of everything. Well...all the fun stuff. Mel has the boring (to me) parts, which makes her happy anyway, so that's a win fucking win. We also had a nice chat about just how systematically Gwen pitted us against each other. Well, Mel against me. They were best friends for ten fucking years. I was too new for her to figure out how to manipulate. Or was I? Maybe all that personal shit was her route. Whatever. Didn't work, skank. You're out. We won. And you don't even know that you're busted. I am taking a great deal of pleasure in the fact that she still doesn't know. Every exchange is so loaded and detached now.

I'm like a child giving her the finger and sticking out my tongue at the back of her head every time she leaves my office. Not metaphorically, either. Actually.

And yes, leaves *my* office...because the seat of power has changed. I don't go to her office anymore. Her smaller, pathetic, not getting paid, traitorous, lying ass office.

.

June

Japan is back in the land of the living and apparently is actually coming here. Funny, Gwen's little plot gave me some pretty good perspective on this 'relationship' of all things.

I don't need him. At all.

I thought for a while that he gave me some sort of strength. Maybe security is a better word. I don't know. I think he was a moment in time, but now it doesn't really work for me. And just like they all do when they sense retreat...now all of the information and sharing is starting to flow.

Thing is, I don't think he's very nice.

I'm noticing now without the obsession and weird longing that he relies a little too much on taking shots at my character. It's always couched in the context of joking about what a snob I am. But I think he's actually invested in taking me down a notch.

Maybe I'm just being overly sensitive. We'll see in a week I guess.

I'm taking the kids to the movies. The boy has voiced his opinion on the inappropriateness of having a gentleman caller in my bed. And now is crying and freaking out and just told me it would be easier if one of us had died.

Probably seems that way.

If I was an actual whore who had a new uncle in the house every week, maybe he'd be happy that there's only one person. Can't say that though can I? Sure can't. Sheltering them is my job, I know...Maybe I've been a little too good at it. Whatever. Therapy has always been a line item in the budget.

And later...in true kid 'how can I manipulate this situation for my benefit' fashion...could you buy me porn...and maybe then could we have the most ridiculous conversation about masterbation? Won't that be so much fun for you, mother?

In his little death scenario, I think it's safe to presume I am the parent that lives.

Jon does not pay me enough for this.

~~~

So here's a new interesting update...Japan's ex has taken to calling and writing and begging him to get back together and then in the next breath telling him that she's not afraid of him anymore, and he doesn't scare her, and his dad hit on her...What the fuck is that? That's some Jerry Springer bullshit. And I don't even want to know the specifics. I draw the line at Springer.

Oh, and there's fucking abuse and mother hate. All of the warning signs are there on full display. So that condescending, put me in my place thing he does to me is not my imagination.

He's a bully. And when I thought it was a joke, I was along for the ride. Now, though, not so much. And there is a part of me, the sucker part, that wants to help him...I hope there aren't bigger horrors in his past—cause ain't no cure for that. None that he'd pursue anyway...Only sorrow and the inevitable next divorce. I should cancel this.

~~~

Are there no normal people on the planet? I'm so fucking agitated. Jon's fat brother wants me to call him...Just fucking pick up your phone and say whatever you need to say. God, I hate that. I'm busy. Don't fucking summon me. Just call without all the dramatic flourishes.

This visit is a mistake. If he wasn't already traveling, I would cancel it.

Did he just whine at me? You have to go to work? What am I going to do all day?

It's literally one day. Go to a fucking museum. Go to a bar. Go to a church mixer and find a wife, bitch...Oh, and that one day is the day before we go to Philly for my first conference because why wouldn't the universe conspire to make this an actual shitshow.

And then, I swear to god I thought I was hearing things...Sure wasn't. I gave him the opportunity to say 'nothing' but nope...He did in fact say exactly what I thought I heard...enema....ENEMA??!!! He read it somewhere. Really? Where? You don't fucking read. Something about bacteria...This is the last entry for a week...the week I may finally lose my mind and fucking kill everyone.

~~~

Week and a half actually. Just dropped him at the airport. If I had even one lingering good feeling, it is now gone. It torrentially pissed rain the entire way. And not to call out the Universe, but it was a little lazy in terms of creative foreshadowing.

Turns out, he is mean. Had a public fight in Philadelphia...which actually was a surprisingly good conference. People like me more/hate me less in person. Or they're just fucking chickenshit when they can't hide behind a phone or a keyboard. Either way. They were all very civilized and polite, and I said no less than 70 times...Nice to meet you. I do know who you are. Nice to put a face to the name...I wouldn't know who you were at all if you played by the rules...Insert flirty I'm not the devil but you might be laugh. Float away. And repeat.

Anyway, he left me in a restaurant in some random neighborhood. Just walked out. I wasn't about to give him the satisfaction over some throw away bullshit I said. I don't even remember what it was. But again, I was having to be better than every one...Get a new line, douche. I finished my dinner and was running the odds on whether I was going to get stabbed on my walk back to the hotel. He was waiting on the sidewalk though. I'm not a complete asshole. I was like oh you are, but leaving me in the dark to die isn't a good look for the promotion board. Then we went to Atlantic City, which is a fucking shithole compared to Vegas. And god knows Vegas has its own specialness. It's maybe the most depressing place I've ever been. Our room wasn't ready because for the first time in the history of New Jersey, the parks department?? was on strike. Who knew they were the casino/hotel people? Probably everyone...I played Hold Em for five hours. I was up 500 for a minute, but eventually lost 300...Fucking poker. There was a hot boy at the table, which could amount to zero...Whole thing was awful. Thank god it was only a night.

Then we surprise flew to Vegas, as one does when one needs to wash away gross energy and start over...ostensibly as my birthday gift because we all know what a big gambler I am.

And on said 'I thought it would be nice for your birthday' trip, on the floor of the casino...this absolutely charming POS human called me a JINX...on the floor of the casino??? And not in a whisper like you might if you were talking to oh I dunno...your girlfriend. Loud. Like you might shriek at a junkie who asked you for money for the fourth time that week...And I'm not sure, but I feel like that word is some gambler superstition kiss of death because the rest of the table looked at me like I had just flung actual shit at them.

I was too stunned to do anything but glare. For an eighth of a second I considered flicking my lit cigarette at his stupid microdick face. I figured security would probably at a minimum have to throw me out for that though, so I just huffed and took my jinx ass to bed. In the morning he came in all manner of exhausted and sorry and no lie flipped a $1000 chip at me and said happy birthday.

I was like 'Really? Was WalMart closed? That's the fucking equivalent of a gift card. And I'm not a fucking hooker.'

But I for sure fucked him, because not getting off does not serve me...And then I got my hooker with a gift card ass dressed and went shopping while he slept all day. Annoyingly though, I did reluctantly have to consider that maybe I was actually jinxing him because he did win 10 grand after I took my leave. Ha...The rest of the trip was fine, meh, whatever. Highlight: I heard the most catchy tune in some random shop...The groom's bride is a whore...Best line ever.

Bottom line? We are not compatible. He thinks I'm an elitist slob who can't 'keep house,' and I think he's a cunt.

Also, who knew Movado made not watches? I bought a watch, but who knew?

July

Hell hot. My absolute favorite. I'm working 7 days a week. Jon is gone...Still. Again. I can't keep track. I don't even know why I bother to write it. I have to get divorced, which changes nothing in practical terms. Found a sitter though, so I can stop feeling guilty about them not doing anything. Which they were perfectly happy with I know, but fuck them. They're pool bound every day now. Also, why am I so fat? I'm not sad anymore. I'm just like fat. The 8 skirt doesn't fit. And that's not gonna work. Pants I can live with because they're all different, but a skirt? No ma'am. And my favorite pretty boy intern is back...So my 7 days a week isn't as painful as it could be.

Trina is coming...god help everyone. She is in newly awakened love...With that fucking artist piece of shit, so I guess it's re-newly. I miss that. That feeling of I'm gonna die if I can't touch him right this minute. Although if she gets caught she is gonna die...cause that husband might kill her.

Lizzie is pregnant. I guess she's in Scotland forever now...Funny what we take for granted. I'm sending her taco seasoning and cherry kool-aid. So weirdly specific, cravings. Guess it's better than gravel.

Where is my period? That is the last thing I need to deal with. Summer here is like perpetual PMS though, so I'm just a constant bitch. Makes it a little harder to tell when I should expect it. It always just shows up. I guess I could keep track, but whatever...Worrying about it isn't going to make it come or not come.

~~~

Oh my god...I just had the best two hours. I love Mel and Lily. We literally just laughed for 90 minutes...I look like I've been ugly crying...And I left like a grown-up who only goes to Happy Hour which is so very new and responsible of me. I still don't have my period but the mean is flowing quite freely from my lips. So it's coming.

Did I just set Lafferty up with Gigi? He's so kind. He's like the anti-Japan.

Why would I do that though? I think they'd get along really well, I guess. And they're both there. And we are clearly just friends.

We just talked for like three hours. I don't get it. I mean I get it, but aren't you supposed to be with the person who feels like your best friend? I'm a little drunk. But I just want them both to be happy, so maybe it will be together. I'm not sure I'm going to enjoy that as a reality, but for now it seems to be a thing I did.

~~~

So Japan, who has been very sporadic in his contact, and who cares, just called and the boy picked up. And when I called him back he said, 'you need to tell your son...' in a tone that shut down my brain.

I'm sorry...What the fuck did you just say to me?

You need to tell your son...

You need to eat me.

And then I hung up. That will not be a thing. Ever. Game the fuck over.

Bleeding and hating.

~~~

This was an awful day. Woke up late. I came down to find a giant red kool-aid stain on the stupid 1950s laminate kitchen counter...and

I flipped my shit. They thought I bought them kool-aid, so they made some...Bitch, I distinctly said it was going to Scotland. Never in your lives have we had kool-aid. And why would you wait til I went to bed to make it? And where the fuck is it if you thought it was really for you? The boy also ate my almonds in their middle of the night frat party shenanigans. Then my admin quit. Then a fucking lawyer screamed at me on the phone for 35 minutes. Loud doesn't scare me and doesn't make you right, motherfucker. That was actually fun though. I got to exorcise some rage. They all think it's the first time I've talked to someone so incredibly smart and important. It might be my favorite thing. Though if I didn't like it, I am definitely not making enough for that kind of fight.

—

And then, because it needed to be better...Japan called. I don't really know why I even answered. I didn't really care to hear anything he had to say. I should have gone with that instinct because it was all manner of bullshit. He doesn't really know me. He doesn't love me. I'm messy. My kids have no discipline. I was like mmhmm...or maybe you hate women, and you should sort your own shit before you tell me what's wrong with me. None of this matters to me by the way, but thanks.

And that was it.

August

The dog ate my almonds. Ten bucks worth. When did almonds get so fucking popular in this house? Can Jon just home and take these kids? I just want a break. I'm so tired of everything. I need a sanity schedule.

~~~

He's back! Thank actual God.

And now we have bees? I hate nature.

~~~

My first day of liberation. I still have a little Japan residual, but it's anger not sadness. He handed me a very clean break. I'm going shopping after work because why not be the cliche. It's better than ice cream. I'm not even upset. Just keeping myself occupied til Trina gets here tomorrow.

~~~

Oy vey...I always thought it was pure luck that we lived through our 20's...If we had had money, we might not have. Cause money makes dinner at the bar with three bottles of wine a little too easy. Just two girlfriends catching up and having some supper. Not that our tab was ultimately an issue because we met a lovely father/son duo. I thought that it was a grandfather/grandson for most of the night.

The kid was cute, so why wouldn't I be innocently chatting the way normal humans do when you're all sitting at a bar eating a full meal and all of the players are pleasant.

I'm not sure when she decided...maybe they decided together, but I had no idea—even though it was totally her MO our entire lives, so shame on me. I still didn't get it when Mr. Burns picked up our tab. Junior was like let him get it. He's got way too much money. I saw the bill. I wasn't sad, but I wasn't super psyched to let that happen. Trina on the other hand, was more than happy to allow said gentleman to pay for our dinner...which should have been my actual clue.

I have to say though, I've seen her do some crazy shit but this one didn't even occur to me. Not til Junior said I guess it's just us now. And I turned around and she was fucking gone. With the old as dirt dude. To his hotel. I was like, ummm...she's not actually a hooker...and no offense to your dad. He seems lovely, but what the actual fuck?

Dude. We laughed for like ten minutes.

So she got the corpse and the good hotel and I got the kid and the ok apartment. She hasn't called yet, so who knows how that went. I gave Junior the number. He's a nice kid. Sex is kind of blurry, but I have an overall good feeling going...And I'm up 250 bucks, so if she's not dead...Actually, if he's not dead, then that's a pretty decent evening.

She's not dead. I'm going to fetch her.

—

All she said was 'don't ask...it was translucent.' I almost puked.

The whores are staying in tonite.

—

That husband called me like 100 times. Apparently last night too, but I haven't really even looked at my phone. I wasn't super nice when I finally answered, but he did have the misfortune of catching me right when I woke up from my nap...and I am never pleasant after a nap.

Dude, you met her before you married her. We went to fucking dinner. Now, we're napping. Calm the fuck down.

He should be more worried about where she is while he's at work.

To be fair, she was not behaving. but he knows I would never tell him a fucking thing. And even if I wanted to, the specifics are so nuts it would just be hurtful. Anyway...she's a bitch and always turns off her phone, if she even knows where it is. Oh my god, she has another secret phone too. This is a dangerous game she's playing. Though, I feel like he gets off on it a little. Cause she's been caught like five times and he's just like why do you do these things? Tell me everything...it's fucking weird. This dude though. This is different. She might really love him...And it's not going to be good.

~~~

Now I need to recover from staying in. He's still calling. She's fucking driving, you complete maniac. My god he's annoying. I'd be fucking everyone too.

I think I might go shopping this afternoon. Ha. Who am I kidding? I'm not moving out of this bed.

~~~

Junior texted. Hi. It's Nick. Thank god...I have to get better with that. One name shouldn't be such a challenge. Pleasantries were exchanged. I did not inquire about the welfare of his father. Having dinner on Thursday. That'll be fun. Maybe. If I recognize him. That's ridiculous. I saw him in the morning. No current recall, but surely I will know him when I see him. That's 'surely' with about 92% certainty. So a B+. Not awful. Not great, but not terrible.

Gigi and Lafferty's date is tonite. I don't think she wants to go. She said she's worried it's going to be weird with our history. I told her there wasn't any history. We're just friends. And truthfully, there isn't anything. Me being in love with him a million years ago is hardly a thing. I fucking fall in love with everyone...He's had a gazillion chances, and he doesn't want anything with me. And that funeral one-off doesn't really count. I don't think I even told her, and I'm sure he's not going to bring it up. Do I feel weird about this? I don't think so.

I might later if it goes well, and they get married.

~~~

Guess who's getting her raise retro'd to June!!! Had dinner with the mothership team. We got pretty much everything we asked for including some hardcore gratitude for saving them 100K from that lying, thieving bitch. Cause they were about to give it to her.

Anyway...new dude likes us. We've already made him look good, and we haven't even tried yet.

Apparently Lafferty and Gig's date didn't go well. She said he spent a lot of it talking about me. And I'm not saying it was spite, but she did 'mention' I was in a semi-serious long distance relationship. That's my bad for not keeping her updated on Japan. But really...do I really even care at this point? He has had ample opportunity...

I got a cleaning lady. And Jake's home.

September

We discovered a big fat backlog of mess that Gwen left. So my workload just tripled, and it all has to be done yesterday. She's so fucking lucky she has an actual baby, or I would drive over there and yank her out of her front door and beat her to death. I get to work all weekend.

In non-murderous news, dinner with Nick tonite. I am so feeling my fashion choice. It's a very early 70s cocktail party with an edgy swinger undercurrent vibe.

Should I pay? I feel like I should pay, since his party treated last time. I have no idea how old he actually is. Or what he really looks like. Or anything about him. I hope I didn't just make him cute in my head.

—

Turns out zero cause for concern. I did recognize him. He is really cute. So not just wasted eyes and wishful thinking. Really young though. I think he said 25. He's very polite and soft-spoken, which is completely at odds with the boy in the bedroom.

I was far more coherent tonite and I gotta say...it was pretty intense. Like dark and dirty...not growling exactly, but sort of. It was like physically a level beyond screaming, but quiet. I don't know what the fuck it was, but I'm pissed that I wasn't more sober the first time. I didn't actually want to leave. I kept saying I had to go, but then I couldn't make myself get up. And it just kept going...

Sex doesn't affect me like this. This is a new weirdness. I feel like I'm in a trance. My face is hot. Am I fucking blushing? Butterflies are different too. It's not the flutter. Not even the wave. It's like a cement rod keeps punching me in the gut. 45 minutes replaying it my head? This is a definite problem. Cause that just happened.

He just texted 'wow' I said 'wow for real'.

~~~

I'm super excited that I get to go try not to be catatonic all day. Frame by frame replay and borderline coma are still in full effect. This isn't normal. Even Diz knows something's up. He's just looking at me. Maybe I'm about to have a stroke and he's contemplating whether or not to get me some orange juice.

Or I've been just sitting here on the edge of my bed for 20 minutes.

Gotta shake this shit off and start to function like a thinking human.

Also, have to do the last of back to school shopping and order Lily's birthday gift...And the girl called to tell me she wants to color her hair. Something drastic I'm sure...she hasn't yet released specifics.

—

Do I want to come over and hang out?

The responsible answer is I have a ton of work to do tomorrow. And I'm so fucking tired. And I'm already in my pajamas...

~~~

He really did want me to hang out...with other people. They didn't stay long. I was polite, but my energy was very much Get The Fuck Out. He is clearly the stand out of that group of whatever they were...friends I guess. Followers maybe...So another contradiction. Nothing about him makes sense outside of that room. Or maybe it all does-just not to me.

I feel like this little escapade is going to be the thing I search for for the next 10 years. Like Goldilocks. Except with dicks. Goldilocks and the 300 dicks. Well Brownilocks...

Regardless, as much as I'm enjoying this hypnotic state, it can't go anywhere. And god knows I can make something out of just about anything. We just have nothing in common. And I'm sure his future wife won't be too down to share him once a week. While it lasts, though...

I'm buying Trina a thank you gift.

~~~

Back To School Night. My favorite. I am so foul today. Those children are back forever, which has put a wrinkle in seeing Nick as often as I'd like. I was going to say maybe that's for the best, but that's fucking nonsense. I drunk bought Nutrisystem and forgot. I thought someone sent me a gift. This shit is gross. But apparently drunk me decided the 8 skirt situation was worse.

Some new marketing dude appeared today from the mothership. Like has an office with no explanation of who he is or what he's doing here. Christopher Pauling. Christopher not Chris. One of those. He seems nice enough, kinda cocky. White bread hockey player. Though anything that triggers my Jake response is probably unholy. And now I'm fucking late.

~~~

Virginfest is today. I'm going shopping. Mel is there. And so is Jake...This is not my happiest of days. I'm having a touch of melancholy. The music thing is a bit of a killer. And I can't shake the feeling that I should be there with him. Oh well...Ain't no Hollywood ending.

—

Or...There totally is if it was a dark as fuck comedy.

He's fat!!!! Already. Not just a little. Pig fucking fat. The fattest he's ever been!!! Ever. Almost unrecognizable...if I wasn't stalking—because yes, I 100% unapologetically totally was—I wouldn't have believed it was him. The universe has done shone down on me. I have never seen anyone blimp up that fast...This is not very yoga, but dammit I am so fucking far out of his league. I will never again pine for his fat ass.

~~~

Doing laundry and still feeling so happy for the first time since it all went down. Which of course makes me immediately feel bad. I'm not proud of taking so much pleasure in his 50 pounds of karma. Because I for sure am, but I also feel a big wave of sad for him. And that is never a safe place.

~~~

Of course he was in the dream. Why can't I let go? Because it's still open? Because for 6 months I lived for Messenger, curtailed my life and was held hostage by that computer. And he's a rat bastard. And all of my hot boyfriend babble...Not today kids. Not anymore. Not hot. Two years and he's gone to hell. That's what happens when you exit the orbit. Fuck his fat ass. Got a thank you card from Movado. So that reminds me...fuck the other one too. I absolutely should have punched him in his face when I had the chance.

I think it's time to see Nick.

~~~

Auditors are coming today. This parent trap is getting old. Oh, and there was a mugging down the street last night?? At knife point. I would be freaked out, but someone got hired to do that because no one can even find this neighborhood when they want to.

~~~

Hottest accountant ever. Maybe Mississippi does have some redeeming qualities. Chemistry and no ring? They're here for a week. I am already tired of having to be appropriate...and the week has just begun. All mothership. All week. Boston gets here tomorrow.

~~~

Shopped for five hours. Bought earrings. Five hours. One pair of earrings.

Had a dream in which Jake appeared at his former size. It was funny to dream about him and not really like him in it...Still love him. Still. What the fuck is wrong with me? I think it's a weird co-dependent thing. He won't let it go with any sort of finality and I can't stay away with any permanence. But I'm always the dumb-ass. And he gets to reject me...I've done pretty well this time. It helps that he's a fucking pig though. That's for absolute certain.

~~~

Done working for other people. I have to do it now. I'm getting old. And I'm foul this morning. Sad foul. Depressed foul. Crazy foul. PMS foul. Hate everyone already foul.

—

Oh my God!!!! That fucker is leaving the website!!! And not by choice. That's what you get you lying, talentless, plagiarizing piece of shit. The universe has given me another gift. First Fatty McFucker and now the boy who stole my job and trashed my name. Justice is sweet. I am drinking beer and going to see Nick.

~~~

Jake wants to go to dinner next week. I didn't answer the email. Gotta help the girl with her homework...Maybe? Fuck...

Gwen just called. Didn't answer that either. I don't want to talk to her. I don't want to talk to Jake. What is this timing? It's a little chilly, so we should reach out and get her on the hook while she's receptive. It's a smart move. I do love fall.

I want Jake to go away. Do I? I have to be done. It's been too long. What would I get from it? Nothing. Even if he wants me, which is only until he gets me...he crushed me. He broke my fucking heart. And I could ask him why. Prolong it. Fuck him even, but it won't make it better. I want to see him. I want to kiss him. But he's not the person I fell in love with. He's the person who went to Iraq and did exactly what he promised not to do. I don't think I will respond. Nothing can make it right. Not Gwen either. I'm going to say nothing to either of them. I'm not feeling super forgiving at this moment.

Which sucks so fucking much because I miss both of them a lot...just not so sure what I miss about either of them was real.

~~~

Set up my first 401K today. Feeling like an actual adult. Christopher offered me a job...He's got a lot of side shit going on. Not my thing, but I'm enjoying him. Dare I say we are about to be best friends? Maybe...

Going out with Nick.

~~~

I am so hungover. We are refiling every fucking piece of paper we have. Which makes me want to die a lot. Totally behind. Gotta get it together.

~~~

Ran out of cabinet space at I. Heard Unbreak My Heart on the way home…Almost cried. Now I'm shitting my brains out and drinking a little wine.

Just had a total urge to call him…

~~~

Don't remember that…feeling like calling him. So more than a little wine…I'm a little anxious this morning. Not a full blown Sunday, but I just had a little freak out like did I send any email? Thank god I did not.

—

And then I did. All I said was 'Why'?

I'm completely spiraling…I seem very calm to look at me. I made it through dinner like a normal mother—engaging and present. And then I got up and very deliberately walked like a serial killer to the computer and just sent it. I don't know what I expect to hear.

Because I'm a spineless cunt who's on a collision course with self-destruction?

Why?

Why am I attached to a phantom? Is the better question.

~~~

Way more vulnerable to complete meltdowns when I'm tired. I wasn't even drinking. Woke up pissed off though, which is better than whining and wallowing. Though, not by much because I'm not sure exactly who or what I'm pissed off at. Probably myself for being so fucking weak. Or because I know today is pay bills day and that always pisses me off. The former more likely.

~~~

How about this radio roundup...No lie. Blurry. I'm The Only One. Crazy. Falling. Heartbreaker. And Blurry again. And two Jake emails that I'm afraid to open. So I won't.

I'm not saying that that playlist was for me. But if the Universe wanted my attention, that's a pretty good poke.

~~~

Saw The Departed with Nick. Really good. First time I've ever liked DiCaprio. It was our goodbye date. He was very cute and very nervous...The girl he's been seeing for a while...blah blah blah. That's not shitty. I knew. We didn't talk a lot, but a shift is a shift. I died a little for him when he said he was sorry but he didn't want to be a liar. He looked like he was about to cry. I'm going to miss him for sure, but I'm happy for him. Happier still that I didn't let that gain emotional traction that I'd have to recover from. Happiest though, that I had the good sense to fuck him before the movie.

~~~

Fired Tony today. Cried in front of my staff when I made the announcement. I was trying not to, but I care about them on a way too personal level. And it was sad. I was sad. And everyone liked him, which mad it sadder. Whatever, they're probably more afraid of me now. Cause we all know how mean I get after I weep. And I did. Missy avoided me all afternoon...after she picked up my lunch and Starbucks. Fear or guilt? Both probably.

I'm drunk. And my hair looks spectacular. Not tonite, Satan.

~~~

Had a weird convo with Lafferty last night. Apparently the girl looks like his niece. Is this a sign? I don't really understand this relationship. Is it because we're friends? I mean, I have male friends. Not a lot of them, but like Marks and I are friends, and we talk about shit like friends. So I'm just confused. I know he's not celibate. I'm not sure it's worth examining. I'm done helping men fix their shit. Just because I'm fascinated by what makes you tick, doesn't mean it's my job to unravel it for you. Figure it out yourself and then call me.

I should call Marks. Every time he answers I'm surprised he's not dead. But he would have no time for this crybaby shit. That's probably why I have strategically not spoken to him for like a year.

~~~

Here's a fun day at work. I pick up my phone to a lovely gentlemen who hates me personally, apparently. Started off with the normal threats. However then his tone changed and he proceeded to read off every address I've ever had, including the current one, rattled off Jon's and my children's names and then call me an Arkansas dummy. I said Ha. That's Alaska. AK is Alaska, not Arkansas, you fucking retard.

I was calm, but I was fucking scared. Called the police. And with that, we crossed some corporate danger threshold. Now we're also moving the office. Dude, jousting with ego-drunk attorneys is sport, but I do not make enough money to take a fucking bullet.

—

So as I was in a fragile state already...I checked the page. He's lost weight. Annoying...Regardless—immediately after, I got an email from him. Further confirming my belief that he is the devil. The devil waits for you to be weak and contemplating your mortality to strike. When you don't have the strength to resist. And I want him to call. I want to see him. Like heroin. And I cannot see him because he will be all I will be able to think about...Again...and I'll be at square one.

I will not do it. We will never be.

I want to see his face. Nope. Stay strong.

Hate-listening to McRae, drinking a little Zin and watching breast cancer shoes on QVC.

~~~

Drank a whole lotta Zin and threw up. And let that be a lesson: Jake = Vomiting. Very expensive vomiting.

~~~

I won the football pool. Contested of course by hateful boys who didn't win. They said I cheated because I offered Curt half of the pot if I won if he'd tend to my team. Which was genius I thought. I can barely remember my name. I'm not about to remember to trade and bench and whatever they fuck they do. They're just mad because they didn't think of it. But I do have the advantage of being the boss, so suck it. Whiners. Seems kinda short though for football. I dunno. Fucking English majors. If I had enough money, I'd be single forever. I found my winter boots because it snows once every three years? Whatever...They're cute. And they're Born. Which is bizarre because I'm not actually down with the hippie earth mother vibe. They feel kind of Alaska though. Except they're not made of actual fur...Gwen sent me an 'I'm sorry, can we talk' text...which is better than expecting me to pick up a cold call. I guess I could talk to her. Big picture, I benefitted from her fuck up.

Ugh...What have we learned about big picture? Big picture is the gateway on the slippery slope that sends us right back to Jake. All the vampires really, but he's always the final destination.

Can I forgive and maintain any sort of boundary? People do that don't they? I'm not feeling so sure of that...I'm not responding.

My skin looks wretched. All dull and splotchy. Probably because there's way less good energy since Nick went away. Duh. I need a new toy.

~~~

So I emailed the accountant. And he responded in about 17 minutes. So we'll see if he wants to play. Long distance I can do. Like a champ. But he is sort of a moving target logistically. It'll be a fun distraction if nothing else.

November

Shopping keeps the Sundays away...spent a little, got a shitload of stuff. Pretty bag and earrings for mommy. Shirts for the boy. Shirts and pants and socks for the girl. They're not home yet, so I have a few hours to sit in peace.

~~~

In inconvenient interruption of time and space news, I have the girl's conference today for 15 minutes. What the fuck is the point? Takes longer to park the car...

~~~

Got a hot cop when I filed my police report. That never happens. Though the cops didn't seem as concerned as I was. They were kinda like we can't really do anything about this...ummm...yeah, no...it's all good...I just want you to have a suspect in case something weird happens. Like I'm murdered. Fucking really...

And Missy straight lied to my face today. Which makes me rethink the Tony thing. Did she let him take the fall for her fuck up? Her days are numbered. The mothership is back in asshole mode. And I got another threat. Not as scary as the subject of today's police report but still...on what planet is fielding multiple threats of bodily harm on the daily in banking a fucking thing?

Oh, and I for sure just met my favorite new person on the planet. It's been a day. We interviewed a new receptionist. This child (like actually 19) from California. This bitch lost power while she was coloring her hair, and she didn't cancel. She fucking came with it soaking wet and was still on time. I am obsessed with her. Moved for a boy, which whatever...haven't we all...No family here. Funny, smart and fearless?? Obsessed. Mel was like calm down. And I was like you're here as a courtesy. Missy was trying to be all professional because she's a conniving, spiteful hooker who hated her on sight. This girl is model pretty, so of course Missy thinks she will make sure her time here is brief. I could feel it. Nope. You're the one that's gonna go, precious.

If we didn't have a brigade of chickenshit lawyers controlling HR, I would have disappeared her already.

~~~

When did all the cars get so soft? They're all so generic now. Like maybe not the Mustang, but then you have to have a Mustang. That's like a second car if I was a douche...Pathfinder maybe. Obviously the Rover, and the GWagon but even them...Jeep isn't super comfortable to drive. This is a ridiculous rabbit hole, but it's annoying...Everything is just fucking blobby and boring.

Just made the boy the best black eye for school. It looks like I actually punched him... And we made blood last night...Fun, but we couldn't have done all of this two weeks ago when it was Halloween? Gotta love the school system. Making shit easy for us.

~~~

The site is two steps away from launch. I just got a serious bug in my ass. And Lizzie has already gotten the framework built. Now printer today and samples will be on their way.

Tomorrow, Missy gets her dose of reality. Fuck that bitch. Lying constantly. If I could prove she set Tony up, I would throw her fat ugly ass in a ditch. She's fucking crazy.

~~~

Jake sent me some bullshit response to that why email. What was that like five months ago? Kidding. I wish. I told him the next time he got the urge to put out the feelers, he should fight it.

You want to talk to me, start with I'm sorry...I'm so over this.

~~~

He called. And stuttered and said he was sorry. And that he just had no regard for me whatsoever while he was there. I did not bail him out. I just let him talk and be uncomfortable. I believe 'embarrassing' and 'humiliating' were the precise words he used. 'Welcome to my world' was the totality of what I said. I was so good. And it was fucking hard. I wanted to rescue him so badly. But I kept my fucking mouth shut.

After he hung up he texted 'That sucked' 'You deserved for that to suck.' 'I know.'

He wants to have dinner on the 4th.

~~~

I'm not sure how I feel about it. I didn't smile and say 'yessss' after I hung up. He did ask how he could make restitution.

Idiot!!! He does this every time. And the fact that you are writing 'every time' should be answer enough. It would be for a sane person.

Gig asked if I thought I could see him and not sleep with him. I don't know the honest answer to that question. I don't know if that's even the issue. Seeing him, fucking him, talking to him, communicating with him at all. They're all equal. The outcome is the same. So much for not allowing 12/4 to creep into my consciousness.

The girl colored my belt with Sharpies. And I have to pay the IRS...I can take no more.

~~~

Will we be 80 and still doing this? I've shut him out of my brain for like the past two days. I can't rally the hope to see him. And that's new...But it's here, so let's see if I can maintain it.

~~~

Jon is MIA and has given me no plan on how they will be getting to his family's. I guess it's time to text that brother. Worthless. Now I'm your fucking travel agent too? It never occurred to me that he wouldn't make it home in time for Thanksgiving. I guess I could take them to Trina's, but I did not mentally prepare either of us for that.

Work is eerily quiet. Missy is behaving because she knows I'm on to her and checking her shit every second. I'm hoping she'll just get fed up and quit. That would be too easy.

Know what's weird...I just realized that laughing until I cry has only really been with my female friends. Trina and I literally just laughed about mustard for 45 minutes. Marks was in my dream last night. Marks always makes me laugh a lot. I should call him. I don't even know if he and Jon talk anymore. Which is sad, but also fine because I should get something good in the divorce for all my trouble.

~~~

Is my house bugged? Jon's back, and he made me laugh last night. So I guess now we're officially girlfriends? Whatever. They're taking Diz too, so I like him more than I did yesterday. His mother is gonna wanna flip. But she can't because he did in fact save her life, so how would that look? Ugh, the one day I tell the girl she doesn't have to go to school, she wants to. I'm getting my period, and I'm so grumpy. I might just cancel my plans. I don't even want to go now.

~~~

And I'm back home to my very quiet kid and dog free house. How they're both still alive is beyond me. That husband is a lot. Though, Trina is so evil. I'm not sure how he hasn't legitimately killed her. She called his mother a cunt...At fucking Thanksgiving. To her face. I laughed before I could even stop it. It was so over the top. There was way too much alcohol. His buddy tried to fuck me in my sleep. Ummm, no rapist. That's not how that works. If I wanted to fuck you, you would have been invited. I'm not going to say I fled, but I was up and gone at first light. Talked to Jake. Gotta love a transition. Look at me being all casual with it...it was though. Logistics really. Dinner is just dinner. Nothing more. Nothing less. I want the chance to sit across from him and he wants...well, I don't know what. He said to put Iraq to rest.

December

Dinner tonite. I don't feel nervous. Probably because I'm not really convinced it's going to happen. I will be going to dinner with or without him, though. And I will look stunning because that's not optional. If it happens, this is just the last thing to check off the list before I move on.

I hope.

—

That. Was. Bizarre. Small talk...until he asked me if he hurt me. And other than a twinge of pity for his obvious discomfort, that was the closest I got to feeling an emotion. Not quite sadness though. Just blinding confused rage...

Did he hurt me????

I think I managed to keep my volume in check. At least that's what I am choosing to believe. I don't remember being able to see or hear anything around us. But I could feel the tears.

Did you hurt me?

Yeah. You ripped my heart out. I never asked you to do anything but not lie to me. Well...and take down that profile. And end that nonsense with the dishrag. How'd that work out by the way? Ugly as I hope?

Yep.

All the music?

Gone. Every bit of it.

Wow. Good for her. I did not think she had that in her.

And then we laughed, and it was ok for a while.

Until the check...

I'm not with any of them.

I just stared at him.

I get that you can't believe me.

Oh, I believe you. Because I've met you. I just don't know that it matters.

Where do we go from here?

I don't know that we go anywhere.

Do you think you can forgive me?

I already have, or I wouldn't be here. (That pause didn't take as long as I wish it would have) I don't like you very much right now, though.

I didn't mean to hurt you.

Yeah well I'd like to believe you didn't set out to, but the end result is the same isn't it? And it's not like I didn't fully participate. Nothing was an accident.

Did you really sleep with him?

(Ahhhh...there it was)

No.

That was fucked up.

I kinda feel like there was more than a little fucked up swirling, so...

I'm sorry.

So am I.

I wasn't though. Sorry I hadn't been worse, maybe.

We kissed in the parking lot for a long time. A really long time. Like my face hurts...

It was the strangest thing though. I still can't quite wrap my head around it...

I felt nothing.

I mean, I was physically there, but I kept thinking how foreign it was...not feeling. This mouth is all you've wanted forever and there's nothing.

I said text me when you get there. He said I'll call...And then he got in the car and drove away.

I sat in my car shaking my head like a dog for ten minutes. Like I was trying to somehow knock the love back into place...

Maybe I really am just finally done. No butterflies. Not a flicker. How does that happen? It's a little unnerving.

~~~

He did call when he got to the hotel, but I was sleeping. I told him about the numb thing though. Just now.

He said he doesn't believe me. There's no one in my life like him. Beyond arrogant.

Oh my god...Wait...

Do they all think that?

Have I done such a good job convincing them all that I couldn't possibly live without them because they're so special? Fuck these men.

Though he's not wrong about the second part. Which is infuriating. God knows I wouldn't survive two of him. I love? him. I'm not even sure it's love. Whatever it is though, it's there there. Like soul level there. But the idea that we're going to somehow magically align...Not this week. I fucking hope this isn't some karmic loop I have to stay in forever.

~~~

It's such a pain having to find a new Nick. And this is such a bad time, so close to Christmas. I invited Lafferty to visit. I don't know why. Maybe because we've been in a relationship for years. And it's easy. Dude though, I just immediately changed my mind. I need to be man-free for a minute. And frankly, if I learned anything from Cutter and Japan, (which is debatable) I can no longer give anyone the time of day who can't man-up for me. Or years of attention? Or that.

I applied for a job in Saratoga. Cause I have some misty romantic attachment to three blocks of a fucking main street and a writer's colony that I didn't go to...I've made worse decisions on less.

Do I love the Toureg?

~~~

Bought my camera. So happy!!! 700 all in. Now I have to go buy Toys for Tots and white elephant gifts. Pattern much? No dick, buy all the things. Whatever. Tis the Season.

And I bought the new Lucky. It's so good. Which is weird because Vogue has been so boring. Maybe I just like that Lucky's not pretending it cares about words. Though I do love the Vogue food dude. Probably because he's actually fucking entertaining. If he goes away, I'm out.

Let's be honest though...Why would this be any different than any of your other co-dependent relationships? You'll just keep bitching and let your subscription auto-renew. Ha. Probably.

I swear to god I was just thinking about that dirty artist boy and Trina called to tell me she got busted. Cell phone records and GPS. Marriage is ridiculous. They can only bother to pay attention when we seem happy. Although this is their normal dance, so I guess it was more of a save-the-date inevitability than an actual we never saw it coming murder-suicide scenario.

That worthless fucker, though...how many of my people will he drag into the gutter with him? There aren't really any of 'my people' left, and no one's really in the gutter...but I'm feeling extra dramatic. Oh, and I finally saw his work...Meh...he's not being invited to Basel anytime soon.

~~~

Oh my god I am so glad I didn't freak out and give my notice because we just got the best lawyer. I say we. He officially belongs to the mothership. But since we have an inordinate amount of legal shit, I'm about to have another best friend/playmate. I'm already obsessed. And not in a creepy, wanna fuck him way. He's so smart for real, not just thinks he is. And funny. And humble, which is generally not my experience with attorneys. I already dig him so I guess if he drinks, he's straight and there's chemistry then it would be my very lucky day.

So maybe like 23% creepy?

~~~

189

Yeah. I asked him out. I mean...Again, in a 77% not creepy, wanna fuck him way...just like welcome to the neighborhood. Logo is on the site. Printer is delivering cardstock samples. And the Christmas diamond commercial is really starting to piss me off. That's an unreasonable overreaction, but if I've noticed it enough to hate it? Fuck off with it already.

Tree's up. Securely. I check now 20 times a day like I have OCD. If only that carried over into literally any other part of my world. Groceries bought. The cap(?) that has been fucking up the vacuum cleaner has been unstuck. I didn't even ask. They'd both lie anyway. And now I'm off. The in-laws get here tomorrow. Both of them. No brother though. At least I haven't yet been made aware of it. I hope not...But I'll have reinforcements for cookies, so I won't wanna slit my wrists ten minutes in.

~~~

Christmas was pleasant. I like the busyness of having people around. Nothing exciting. No stand out gifts. No weird sex with Jon. They're still here. I'm going to work tomorrow to hang out with Mel. I'm not really going to do any work. But I'm exhausted. The husband requires a lot of energy—force laughing at every not funny thing that comes out of his mouth. And he's never not talking. It's too much. So I figure I should go somewhere before I punch him in the throat and scream 'For five minutes...Please for the love of all that is holy please please please shut the fuck up!' in his face. Cause 'For five minutes' flew out last night and I'm not sure how long I will be able to stop the rest of it. I mean if he was even remotely pleasant to look at, but nope...I can't think for too long about how she ever let that put its dick in her...Lots of alcohol that's how. Fucking gross.

~~~

Ummm yeah...so I'm sitting at my desk today half-ass thinking about (but not actually) throwing away the thousands of post it notes that are the entirety of my professional organizational system...and I see this flash of a giant human roll by my door. And since I'm low key ready to be gunned down at any minute, I'm way more alert than I used to be...I was trying to be all super casual when I asked Mel if I was seeing things.

Missy's brother. You know, the one she's in love with...Ha. She's a snarky bitch. I laughed way too loud though because it's true.

And then like half an hour later, Missy's in my face bouncing up and down like an actual puppy. Do you have a second? I wanted you to meet my brother.

I know I actively rolled my eyes. Probably my whole head.

But I felt it...

I know intellectually that she said This is Andrew, like any person who has a modicum of social awareness, but it was all manner of far away and Charlie Brown teachery...because...yep...

Before he even made it through the doorway I felt it...

The mf-ing thunderbolt.

This is gonna be sooooo bad.

Fuck. Me.

~~~

Don't miss out!

Visit the website below and you can sign up to receive emails whenever Michelle Marie publishes a new book. There's no charge and no obligation.

https://books2read.com/r/B-A-JSSX-OZLHC

BOOKS 2 READ

Connecting independent readers to independent writers.

About the Author

A wannabe tap dancer (if your feet didn't have to move so damned fast), Michelle Marie is a writer, stylist, photographer, professional talker, and the HBIC at InsideOut Media.

Michelle hails from Pittsburgh, is no relation to Warhol, Carnegie, Aguilera or Porter, but claims the Steelers, Pens and Pirates as her ride or dies.

Read more at https://thatinsideoutchick.com.

About the Publisher

InsideOut is an independent publisher based in Pittsburgh, PA.

www.ingramcontent.com/pod-product-compliance
Lightning Source LLC
Chambersburg PA
CBHW020658030726
47498CB00002B/558